when he's WILD

NEW YORK TIMES BESTSELLING AUTHOR
LISA RENEE JONES

ISBN-13: 979-8725663181

www.lisareneejones.com

Characters

Adrian Mack—34, goatee, dark wavy hair, six-foot-one. Hero of the story. Former FBI agent. Was once undercover with the Devils biker gang, and is now set to testify against Nick Waters, the leader of the gang. Now a prominent member of Walker Security.

Priscilla "Pri" Miller—32, brunette, blue eyes. Heroine of the story. Assistant District Attorney. Used to work for her father's law firm before she decided she wanted to put away the bad guys instead and went to work as an ADA.

Rafael—Younger brother to Adrian Mack. Rock star Latin singer.

Blake Walker—One of the three owning members/brothers of Walker Security.

Lucas "Lucifer" Remington—Walker Security team member. Blond, tattooed, rock god type looks. Pilot.

Savage—Walker Security team member. Former surgeon and special ops.

Dexter— Walker Security team member.

Adam— Walker Security team member.

Kirk Pitt— FBI agent, was undercover with Adrian. Handsome face, big and broad.

Ed Melbourn—District Attorney. Pri's boss. 50's. Fit, a big man, with thick salt-and-pepper hair, broad shoulders, and a broader presence. Single. Ex-military.

Nick Waters—King Devil, club founder, 42, brutally vicious, sports a dark beard with hints of gray, but doesn't drink or do drugs. He just peddles drugs, weapons, and women, while pumping iron, and adding new tattoos. Green eyes.

Grace—Pri's co-worker. 30, blonde, green eyes, in a relationship with Josh, shy.

Josh—Used to be the detective for the DA's office, but now has turned to private sector work. In a relationship with Grace. Light brown hair, strong, classically handsome features.

Jose Deleon—Waters' right-hand man, his assassin, most likely responsible for the murders of the witnesses.

Cindy—Newest ADA, straight out of school, petite, feisty, pretty blonde.

Logan Michaels—Pri's ex-fiancé, works with her father still. blond pretty-boy, clean-shaven jaw. Cheated on Pri with her secretary.

Shari—DA's office receptionist.

Mr. Miller—Pri's father. Owns his own firm. Pri used to work for him, Logan still does.

Mrs. Miller—Pri's mother. Wants Pri to come back to their family firm, refused to go out of town to stay safe during the case Pri is working on.

Chapter One

ADRIAN

I should have Pri on a plane, getting the hell out of Texas right now.

That's what my gut is telling me. That's what every part of me is telling me. Instead, I'm in a surveillance van with Blake and Lucifer outside Pri's favorite Italian restaurant while she's inside at a table, waiting for her parents to join her. They're late now by ten minutes, and her father doesn't strike me as a man to be late.

And so, the three of us just sit in this cracker jack box like sardines waiting for the top to explode. And that's exactly what it feels like my world might do tonight: explode.

We *should not* fucking be here.

I remind myself that just as I want to protect Pri, I'm doing this *for* Pri, taking a risk with her, for her, and because I get why she needs this. She wants to convince her parents to go into hiding, despite knowing they are most likely being bought and paid for by the King Devil, Waters himself. The very man Pri is trying to convict for countless crimes, while I await my role as a star witness. Despite this, ironically, because of all of this, she's afraid for her family. She loves her parents. The problem is that I know how love can flow in one direction.

I loved my brother. I would have died for my brother before he made me kill him. It came down to him or me. I knew he'd choose himself. I always knew. But we, as human beings, need to save those we love. We have to try. I can't deny her the chance to save her parents now before we leave, because when she disappears—and she will tonight—they *will* become targets. At the very least, their safety will be leverage to lure her out of hiding.

But all of that doesn't change one thing: we're tempting the devil tonight, the King Devil, daring Waters to kill us both before we destroy him at trial— the beautiful, fearless ADA and the former FBI agent willing to testify against him standing in his face and daring him to kill us.

I'm leaning over Lucifer's shoulder as he manages the audio feed from Pri's bracelet and pairs it to the camera feed we've set-up both inside and outside the restaurant when Logan walks to the door of the restaurant. Logan is Pri's ex, who works for her father, and by all indications, has been corrupted by Waters right along with her parents, most likely before her parents. He's dirty as sin, a man who'd hurt Pri to save himself. I'm already reaching for the door, intending to go beat his ass and save my woman, when Blake grabs my arm. "Stay the fuck here."

"I will not let him hurt her."

"I know you love her, man," he states. "You don't even have to say it, but that means you need to stay alive to stay with her. Adam is inside with her. And so is our man Beckham. He flew in tonight to be here for you. You trust them both."

"I barely know Beckham," I say of the sudden new addition to this mission, if that's what you want to call my life at present. "I've worked with him once before tonight. That's not enough for me to say I trust him."

"He tells me you saved his life overseas. He says he owes you. Let him pay you back tonight. And as for trust. You *trust me*. That's not a question. I trust him. And *you,* asshole, *you* are not getting out of this van and ending up in a jail cell where Waters will have you murdered."

I draw in a breath and lower my hand from the door. "If anything happens to her—"

"It won't," Blake states. "We won't let her get hurt."

I inhale and huddle behind Lucifer again, watching the feed on his screen as Logan walks through the restaurant and sits down across from Pri. I'm remotely aware of Blake squatting next to Lucifer, but I'm not focused on him. I'm focused on Pri. I'm not pleased with the view. I can't make out her facial expressions. "Can you get closer?"

"No," he says. "Camera placement is off."

"That's why we have a man at a table to her left and right," Blake states.

Lucifer holds up a finger and listens a minute, before eyeing me and Blake. "She just told him to go fuck himself," Lucifer says, lifting a hand in our direction and tapping his headphones. "Paraphrasing, of course," he adds, "but that's what she wanted to say. He sat down, told her he was there at her parents' request and that they wanted her to drop the case. She said no."

"And now she's getting up," I say, "She's leaving."

My relief is short-lived as Lucifer expands the view and homes in on a bald man near the entrance of the restaurant. The same man we'd seen visit Pri's father via Blake hacking their security footage. A man we believe works for Waters. Adam steps between Pri and the bald man and closes in on the bald man. Pri smartly halts and turns on her heel, fleeing toward the bar area in the rear of the restaurant.

"The bathroom is to the side of the bar," Lucifer says. "If we're lucky, and she's as smart as I think she is, she's about to lock herself inside the bathroom and stay there until we come for her."

"That's exactly what she'll do," I say, confident Pri is indeed smart and better yet, she has common sense, but she needs backup. Adam's now distracted. And distract and then attack is exactly how Waters operates. "Where the hell is Beckham?"

Lucifer shifts the view, and Beckham, who is at a table on the opposite side of the restaurant from Adam, is standing, about to make a move when a waiter holding a tray of food literally trips and falls into him. *Distract and attack*, I think. "That was no accident," I say.

Blake must agree because he says, "I'm going in," moving toward the door, but pointing at me. "Stay here or I swear I'll kill you for them." He exits the van and shuts me back inside with Lucifer.

It takes all the discipline I own not to follow him. But damn it to hell, he's right about the risk of me being arrested. It's not an accident that Logan is here and Logan is the one who helped trump up an arrest warrant against me for killing my brother. And he did so for one reason: to get me in jail and kill me before I can testify against Waters, the King Devil.

This could be a trap.

It most likely *is* a trap.

One Pri's parents helped set, even if done so indirectly and unintentionally, or at least her father did. He's the one who acts like yet another King Devil and treats Pri like a servant.

And I thought my brother was a bastard.

We'd already be on a plane out of this city and to someplace safer, but Pri was worried about her family. She's here to convince her parents to go into hiding. And what does she get in exchange for her concern? *This shit.*

I force my gaze back to the camera and watch Pri disappear behind the bar into a hallway. All should be well except for one thing: Logan follows her.

"Fuck," I curse, scrubbing a hand through my hair. "That's it. I don't trust that bastard. I'm going to get her." I head for the door.

"You're an idiot," Lucifer snaps as I slide the door open. "At least use the rear exit door in the alley which protects you from the cameras, but that's about all. This is a trap, Adrian. Someone is waiting on you back there."

"Let's hope it's Deleon," I say of Waters' right-hand man, who also plays the role of assassin. "I deserve a second chance to wipe him off the face of the earth."

Lucifer tosses a random baseball hat at me, most likely a part of Adam's arsenal of disguises. "Wear that," he orders. "You still look like you or your popstar brother, asshole. Not a good way to blend in. You're on the run. Act like it. Shave the goatee and that mass of hair on your head. Or at least dye it. Do something to hide."

"You sound like a nagging mom," I say, snatching up the hat where it now lays by my feet. It's already on my head and pulled low, when he adds, "And you're the little bitch that turned me into my mother."

But I've already tuned him out. Saving Pri is all that I can think of right now.

I hop out of the van and shut Lucifer inside.

Discretion means exuding confidence and blending with the crowd. I shut the van door and my weapon stays at my side, hidden by the light jacket the fall season allows me to utilize for cover. I don't even think about pulling it. Not yet. Instead, I walk from the side street to the restaurant parking lot and do so with the stride of a man who knows he's got a great meal and a pretty woman waiting on him. As the door draws near, there's no sign of Adam or the bald man. At the right moment, I pretend as if I've just remembered something in my car. I turn back and then duck low behind a car, and inch a path to the side of the building.

In a few beats, I'm scanning the dimly lit alleyway to find no one in sight. That doesn't mean no one is here, but it's good enough for me right now. I need to get to Pri. I break toward the door, open it, and step into the hallway. Logan isn't there. The bathroom door is shut.

Fuck.

He's in the bathroom with Pri.

Not for long, I think, walking toward the door.

Even if that means I have to blow the doorknob off.

A figure rounds the corner from the direction of the restaurant, and I look up to find Adam headed in my direction. The rear door opens and the bald man appears. "I got this," Adam says, already charging past me. I don't argue. The bald man is his to do with what he pleases.

Logan is mine.

Chapter Two

PRI

It all happened so fast. One minute I was sitting at my favorite Italian restaurant, waiting on my parents to join me. A night that might sound and appear simple, even pleasant, but nothing about me with my parents is ever simple or pleasant.

Meanwhile, members of Walker Security had been nearby, monitoring the situation, watching and listening to me through a tiny recording chip embedded in a bracelet. Adrian was close. He'd wanted me to just leave, to escape with him and there is nothing I would rather do. I love that man. I love him so much and I barely know him. Maybe it's all about the danger and the insanity of being hunted, but we have crashed into each other like two waves that collided into something far more magnificent than when we were apart.

And no one in my life has ever made me feel as if I was stronger with them than apart.

But he does.

And no one in my life has ever put my needs first.

But he does.

Thus, the plan.

I was to confront my father over his involvement with Nick Waters, the King Devil of the Devils motorcycle club, and then to convince him that the game was up. Waters will do anything to survive, to get out of jail and stay out of jail, and that includes murder. Our murders. Waters will kill me and my parents, and most certainly my star witness, Adrian Mack, if he's given the chance.

But my parents didn't show up to dinner.

Logan, my ex, who works for my father, who I believe is the man who connected my father to Waters in the first place, was suddenly sitting in front of me. He claimed that my parents wanted him to "get me under control." By control, he'd meant for me to drop the Waters case, which would surely delay the trial. Which in turn, would surely, for many complicated reasons, allow Waters to walk free.

Sitting there across from Logan, it was hard to know if my father, or my mother, were involved in Logan's appearance. Walker had found some evidence that suggested my father may have been blackmailed by Waters, or perhaps Logan. Or my father could have simply refused the dinner date my mother and I set-up, and Logan had found out, and invited himself to join me. Or not. As I said, it's hard to know what is really going on. My father's firm makes big money protecting bigger criminals. Logan has some involvement directly or indirectly with Waters, and that means so does my father.

Perhaps the daughter in me prefers to believe the blackmail avenue because it's easier than accepting my father as a man who would break the law, rather than simply manipulating it within its legal liability.

But it doesn't matter who's behind Logan trying to get me "under control."

I will not allow Waters, a man connected to murder, drugs, weapons trafficking, rape, as well as sex slaves, to walk free. There is no way I'll let the witnesses who have died trying to make it to Waters' trial, die for nothing.

I'd said as much to Logan. I'd refused to drop the case.

Again.

And with that refusal, I'd left Logan at the table, but I'd spied a suspicious man at the front door. A man I knew from a video Walker Security had shown me. This man had visited my father, perhaps blackmailed him, I can't be sure. Whatever the case, he was someone I knew to fear. But Adam had been there, in disguise, one of Walker's men, protecting me. He'd headed for the man. I'd gone in the other direction.

I'd hurried to the bathroom, giving Walker security a chance to clear my path. I'd thought I was being smart. Until Logan had entered the single-stall bathroom behind me, locked the door, and now we're in that moment.

Chapter Three

PRI

It's as if time is standing still.

Logan charges toward me, rage in his face. The small single-user bathroom shrinks even smaller and I try to back-up, to put space between me and him, but I'm already against the wall. Adrenaline surges through me, and it's not my friend either. It's acid burning through logical thought and creating unsteadiness in the hand that now grips my gun inside my purse. I don't want to pull my weapon. I know my training. You never pull unless you intend to shoot.

I don't want to shoot.

But as an Assistant DA fighting crime in my own way, and the daughter of a father who defends criminals, I have trained and prepared myself for it, if I have to.

"Stop!" I shout at Logan, holding out my free hand for emphasis. "Stop now."

It's too late. He's in front of me, grabbing my hair, yanking me to him. I gasp, shocked by the bite of his hand and the bite of his action. I shouldn't be. He's never been gentle. In fact, he's been far from gentle, a truth that was one of the many reasons we broke up.

"You fool," he growls, his face so close that I can feel his hot breath on my cheek. "You don't fuck with Waters. You're going to get us all killed. Where is Adrian Mack?"

"Let go of me, Logan," I order, my voice strong, forceful even. I'm afraid, yes. I am. But I'm also the woman willing to look the King Devil in the eye and tell him I want him to rot in jail. I will not cower. "Let go now."

He yanks harder on my hair and I slap his face hard and fast. He grabs my wrist, and in that moment, I'm thankful I have never let go of my weapon. But still, I don't pull it. I resist, but just barely. "Where the fuck is Adrian Mack?" he demands.

"I don't know," I snap.

"Bullshit. You know. You're fucking him, which is insanity. He's the reason you're going to get your parents killed."

"I do believe that honor is yours, Logan," I snap. "You're the one involved with Waters."

"You're the one trying to put him in jail."

"He *is* in jail," I remind him. "Where I'm starting to believe you belong."

His eyes burn with anger anew, his energy knifing me with its intensity. "If you want your parents to live," he replies, his voice low, lethal now, "tell me where he is."

"Is that a threat?" I challenge, and with that challenge, I'm buying time, praying someone comes for me. They will. Walker will come. I just don't know if they can get inside the bathroom. And Lord, please do not let Adrian come rushing after me, not when Waters is behind the warrant for his arrest. Waters wants him to be arrested, in jail, where he can have him murdered.

"It's not a threat," Logan snaps. "It's the cold, hard reality of playing in the wrong playground, sweetheart. I tried to get you out before it came to this, but you just wouldn't listen."

A new rush of adrenaline hits me with a strong dose of fear and not for myself. "Where are my parents?" I demand.

"Waiting for me to call and put their minds at ease. Drop the case. Hand over Adrian Mack."

I force myself to be logical again, to remember that Walker Security is watching over my parents even if they don't know it. Walker will protect them. "Adrian Mack trusts no one, which seems to be a smart decision," I say. "I don't know where Adrian is and even if I dropped the case, the DA is ready to proceed without me. Now let go of me."

He cackles out a laugh. "You think Ed will continue without you? That's the funniest thing I've heard outside of you fucking Adrian Mack." He leans in closer. "You need to drop the case and get close to me again. That's the only way you convince Waters you're not a threat."

"We're over, Logan. We've been over for ages."

"I'm done letting you punish me. I fucked someone else. Now you have, too. It's over. You belong to me. You belong *with* me. And this is how this works. You will walk out of here with me. We will go home and fuck. Now. Agree."

Chapter Four

PRI

The very idea of me with Logan curdles in my stomach about as well as sour milk.

That will never happen and yet I *know* I need to buy time for help to arrive. I *know* I should pretend to do as he orders. I should give him the agreement that he demands. That's how I get out of here without either one of us getting hurt. I have to play the game. I know all of this and yet, I can't get the words of agreement to come out of my mouth. And then *his mouth* is on *my mouth*, his tongue thrusting past my teeth, his breath suffocating me. I shove against his chest, desperate to free myself, and to no avail. His hands are all over me, his legs squeezing my knees, capturing my legs, and damn it, I can't get free. I struggle, I fight. I am unworthy of him in strength.

I can't get to my gun. My hands are trapped between his body and my own. But I do the next best thing.

I bite his tongue.

Hard.

He growls and tears his mouth from mine, anger raging in the face I'd once thought handsome and now see as nothing but ugly. He twists my hair in his hand

and pulls with such force that I scream. But he is already kissing me again, swallowing my cry for help, which is exactly what my scream is. Fight or flight kicks in and at this point, there is only one option. Somehow, I free my hand just enough to reach in my purse and pull my weapon, planting it against his gut. "Back up or I'll shoot."

On some level, I realize there's knocking on the door. I'm not even sure how long it's been happening. The room is white noise and still, I say, my voice quaking as I do, "Let go or I'll shoot, Logan."

"Bullshit," he snaps. "You won't risk going to prison. And if you shoot me, you *will* rot in jail. I'll make sure of it."

He leans into the steel of the gun, daring me to pull the trigger, confident enough that I won't pull the trigger that he doesn't even try to take the gun from me. He yanks my hair again and leans into me—his mouth is on my mouth and oh God, I *want* to shoot him. But shooting him and killing him are two different things. At this angle, I *will* kill him. I can't kill him. I'm forced to lower the gun. He smiles against my mouth, pure smug satisfaction, pinning my shoulders with his, essentially ensuring I cannot lift the gun again. He yanks my dress up, and then his hand is between my thighs, shoving under my panties. I'm trapped, completely trapped. I should have killed him. God, I should have killed him.

The room spins and I try to squirm, try to get away, try to lift a knee, and fail in every effort. I need him off me. I need this to end. For a moment, I go blank, and then, I have no idea how, but I'm back in a moment I'd shared with Adrian.

His hand slides to my purse, resting on top. "Is your gun inside?"

"*Always,*" I assure him.

"*Good,*" he approves. "*We both need to know that you can blow a hole in someone's shoe, someone who might or might not be named Logan, and back him the fuck off if you need to.*"

My lips curve. "*In his shoe?*"

"*Losing a toe freaks a person out. Never forget that.*"

"*I'd laugh,*" I say, "*but I don't think you're joking.*"

The memory fades into the present and it's left me both informed and motivated. My legs are still pinned. My arms are stuck by my sides. I have to make this stop and Logan's hands are all over me, his tongue choking me, stealing my voice. I shift the gun in my hand and aim for where I think his foot is. My heart leaps, and adrenaline consumes me. It's almost too much for me to breathe, but still, my finger pulls the trigger. The weapon jerks in my hand with the force of the discharge. Logan is now screaming and he stumbles backward, blood spurting from his foot, my aim apparently right on target. Somehow, I remain calm and I shove my gun into my purse and run for the door. With a shaky hand, I unlock it and yank it open to find Adrian is right there, grabbing me, pulling me into his arms in the doorway.

For a moment, *just a moment*, I forget the danger he is in by being here, I forget how easily he could be murdered, or even arrested and then murdered in a jail cell. His body is big and warm, a shelter in a storm of torment. I draw in his spicy scent, drown in just how good he feels.

I don't want to let him go and it's him, in fact, that pulls back, searching my face. "Are you okay?" he demands urgently, his dark eyes etched with worry, with more torment than usual.

"Yes," I say, and in that moment, all I can think is that I love everything about this man. His dark good looks. His strength, and even the torment that lives inside him and quite possibly destroys him a little more every day, and me with him, but there's a moan from the bathroom that forces me back to the moment where I belong and I amend that statement, "I'm okay, but Logan isn't. I shot him in the foot. He needs medical attention."

Another loud groan bellows from behind me and worried that Logan might actually bleed to death—I'm not a killer, I don't want Logan to make me a killer. I twist around in Adrian's arms, and with him on my heels, step fully back into the bathroom. I gasp as we find Logan shirtless and trying to use his garment to tie off his foot. He glares up at me, and then Adrian, who has pulled the door shut and is now by my side.

"Like fuck you didn't know where he was," Logan snarls. "He's a killer. He killed his brother. And he'll fuck you to the finish and then kill you, too."

The words cut and punch and I glance at Adrian to find his spine stiff, the tight press of his lips accented by his dark goatee. Logan starts shouting profanities at Adrian and I honestly don't know how the man is speaking right now, for the pain he must feel, but shock is a powerful thing.

Adrian doesn't react to the onslaught of words, at least not with comment. He moves toward Logan and unsure of his intent, I'm preparing to act, to intervene. Adrian kneels beside Logan. I'm instantly right behind him, about to go to my knees, but I never get the chance. Logan curses at Adrian again and then takes a swing at him. I gasp as Adrian catches Logan's hand, and then shoves Logan to his back. He doesn't even punch Logan, but somehow Logan seems out of energy, unable to get up, thank God. Adrian grabs Logan's shirt, ripping it into pieces and I understand his intent now. That shirt will be used to wrap Logan's wound properly and stop the bleeding. Adrian's trying to save Logan's life, despite the fact that there is no question that if the situation were reversed, Logan would leave him for dead.

Yes, Adrian killed his brother, but I have never been more certain that in that moment that he had a reason, an unavoidable, critical reason.

"What the hell, Adrian?"

At the sound of Savage's voice, who is both a wild-ass crazy person and a doctor, relief follows. I whirl around to find him—big, thickly muscled, a scar down his face—consuming the doorway behind us. He moves quickly past me and kneels next to Logan and Adrian.

"You cannot be here, dweeb," Savage continues, focused on Adrian. "You need to get the fuck out of here."

"Who the fuck are you?" Logan demands of Savage, and then he starts cursing at him. Savage reaches inside the leather bag at his hip, pulls out a syringe of some sort, injects Logan, and Logan is out instantly, eyes shut, voice now silent.

"I got this," Savage says, refocused on Adrian, even as he's pulling supplies from his bag. "An ambulance is on the way. That means the police, too, fucktard. Get the hell out of here before you end up arrested and dead in your jail cell. And take your woman with you."

Adrian lowers his head to speak to Savage, and I don't know what he says, but Savage nods. A second later, Adrian is on his feet, closing the space between me and him, capturing my hand. "Let's go."

LISA RENEE JONES

"*You* go," I say, digging in my heels, my hand pressed to his T-shirt-clad chest. "I shot him. I have to give a statement. I have to stay—"

His hand cups my neck. "Waters will have you killed, maybe tonight. I'm not letting that happen. *We* go now."

"No time for the good girl assistant DA right now," Savage snaps. "Get the fuck out of here!"

He's barely spoken the words and Adrian has my hand, leading me out of the bathroom, and doing so with a force and pace that leaves me no further room to argue. He turns us right, and away from the dining room, toward the rear of the building, down the narrow hallway, but not before I spy Adam blocking the path right. That's why we're still alone. Walker is controlling the traffic to the bathrooms. In a flash, Adrian's pushing open the exit door, and we're leaving the building to enter a dark alleyway open left and right with a fence several feet directly in front of us, an old car sitting beside it. Suddenly sirens pierce the air and police cars are coming from either direction.

"Oh God," I murmur, and my mind is on the trumped-up arrest warrant for killing his brother that we all know is meant to get him in jail, where Waters will have him murdered. I tug on Adrian's hand with all my force. "It's a setup. Waters will have you murdered in jail. You have to go. Leave me here. I'll cover for you. Go over the fence."

"That's exactly where *we're* going," he says, scooping me up in front of him and all but bulldozing me toward the fence, but it's too late. The sirens are loud, right on top of us now. There's not enough time for me to get over that fence, not without Adrian sacrificing himself. I won't let him do that.

I rotate to face him, hands planted on his chest. "I have Walker with me. I'll handle the police. Go! Go! Go!"

"Pri, damn it." The first car halts near us and the minute that officer gets out of his vehicle, if he's dirty, he could shoot Adrian and blame the warrant. They won't so easily get away with killing me. Decision made, with all the speed and effort I can muster, I roll away from Adrian and run toward an officer.

Adrian curses, but I hear the slam of his foot on the metal of the car. I can almost see him in my mind's eye, the torment in his handsome face as he vaults the fence and leaves me behind.

But I'm not tormented.

He's gone. He's alive and safe. I can breathe again.

ADRIAN

I land on the opposite side of the fence, directly in front of a dark warehouse. My fingers press to the grassy area left behind from when this area was a field not part of a cityscape, trees clustered around me, hiding what I feel from my line of sight: I'm being watched. I'm not alone.

I squat behind a wide, old tree trunk and listen to the dull hum of music lifting in the night air, muted voices, telling me the sound comes from a nearby bar. The sound of cars, a distant horn, more voices. And the barely-there snap of a twig.

Sixty seconds ago I thought Pri was better off here with me and I haven't changed my mind.

A dirty cop is harder to kill than an asshole in the woods.

I shift and ease around the tree, just in time to catch a glimpse of movement by the building. A figure in all-black breaks for an industrial trashcan, followed by not one, but two more men. There's another snap of a twig to my left. I decide Pri is better off on the other side of the fence, where Walker will protect her. Right now, I'm at least four against one.

Chapter Five

PRI

I'm panting as not one, but three, police officers surround me, the breathlessness I feel no doubt a mix of exertion and fear for Adrian. He's over the fence, he's safe, I tell myself again, but doubt creeps in. What if someone was waiting for him on the other side? What if the police follow him and find him?

"Ma'am, what is going on?" a short, dark-haired, slightly pudgy, cop demands, his hand on his weapon.

"I'm Pri Miller with the DA's office," I breathe out, not really sure what to tell them first. It's a lot. So very much, in fact, and so I just do my best. I say it all. Who I am. Who Waters is. Why I have private security. How and why I was attacked tonight and by who. I spill it all out in about twenty seconds.

Footsteps clunk on the car behind us, the one by the fence, and I turn to find several officers piling over the fence. There are at least ten officers here, I realize in that moment, and alarm bells go off. Why are there *so many* officers? I rotate to face the three cops huddled around me.

My hand grips my purse, where my gun still sits beyond the zipper, and at this point, I fear I might need it all over again. Not all of these men are not dirty. "Isn't this response a little extreme?"

"We're just doing our jobs," one of the officers explains.

"Exactly." A tall, muscular man, another uniform, steps into the circle. His hair is dark, his skin sunbaked. There's an edge to him, a threatening undertone to his presence and he's only spoken one word. "We have a restaurant full of people to protect and you are the Assistant DA on a high-profile case, worthy of a big response," he adds and eyes my purse. "Is the weapon you used to shoot your ex-boyfriend in that purse?"

My ex-boyfriend.

That phrase does not sit well. This cop knows it, too. He's an asshole and it's intentional.

Still, I simply state, "It is."

Asshole cop motions to another officer, who holds out a bag toward me. "The entire purse please," the officer requests.

I hesitate, resisting handing over my purse, but I drop it in the bag.

"Do you have a license to carry?" asshole cop, the one obviously in charge, asks.

"I do," I reply. "It's in my wallet."

His lips press together and he motions for the officers near us to move away. They do so immediately. Now the cop is toe-to-toe with me, close, too close for professional comfort. Which is what he wants me to feel. He's trying to intimidate me. Because he knows who I am, or rather, who I am to Waters. I eye his badge and then him. "How do you know Nick Waters, Officer Martin?" I challenge, my voice steady now, my courtroom calm sliding into place, the quake in my belly and my hand, gone.

He arches a brow. "What makes you think I know Waters?"

"Don't you?"

"I do not," he replies.

"You know *of* him," I counter.

"I know you shot your ex-boyfriend tonight," Officer Martin says, avoiding my question.

"In the foot," I say. "I didn't want to be raped, but I also didn't want him to end up dead."

"Raped," he states flatly "Can you prove that?"

"*Can I prove that?*" I reply. "Is that how the police department treats victims now?"

"He's bleeding," he states. "You are not. Can you prove what happened tonight?"

"Actually, yes. I'm wearing a recording device. It's all on audio. My security team will happily provide you a copy."

He studies me a moment, a quirk to his lips. He's amused. I just told him I was nearly raped and he's freaking amused. I want to shoot him in the foot. Fortunately for him, I don't have my weapon.

"We understand you're involved with a witness on your case. Adrian Mack is wanted for murder. I assume that was him who went over the fence."

I'm already in my calm place. He can't rattle me. I'm still wearing the bracelet. Walker is still listening to every word I say and I count on them to follow me where I'm about to take them to protect Adrian.

"That was Blake Walker of Walker Security, the company that handles my private security," I say, using Blake because he's here tonight and he shares Adrian's dark good looks. "He got me out of the restaurant after my attack, but he saw someone behind the fence." I hug myself and eye the officers climbing back over the fence, and offering a shake of their heads to the officer questioning me. "I'm actually quite worried about him. He should be back by now."

At that well-timed moment, thank you Lord, Blake climbs over the top of the fence. *Thank God.* The rear door of the restaurant opens and Adam, now wearing a Walker Security T-shirt, steps out into the alleyway. More relief follows. But my relief does nothing to calm the situation. The officers all freak out with men coming at them from both directions, pointing weapons left and right and even at me. My eyes go to Blake as he holds up his hands and says, "Blake Walker. I'm working for the DA and providing personal protection for Ms. Miller. The man that just exited the restaurant is on my staff."

Officer Martin, who'd all but accused me of harboring a fugitive, shouts over his shoulder at another officer, "Call it in." Even as he does, he's pulled his weapon, charging toward Blake.

Chapter Six

PRI

Blake holds his ground as Officer Martin charges toward him.

Holding my breath, I wait for the war to erupt that doesn't occur. Officer Martin halts in front of Blake and there's murmuring—not shooting. They're actually holding a conversation that I can't make out. Blake is eventually allowed to reach into his pocket and produce his ID. Postures seem to relax and so I relax a tiny bit. That's all. I'm still not sure what is really happening.

It takes a full five minutes before some semblance of real calm evolves. To me that means Blake and Adam both join me in a huddle with Officer Martin, but the punching bag mentality of Martin is not over. He eyes Blake. "Tell me again. What the hell were you doing climbing the fence?"

"As I stated," Blake replies. "I saw someone on the other side of the fence and I feared they had a gun."

"And you left her alone," Martin states dryly.

"Not alone," Adam states. "She had me and a team of men watching and listening."

The officer glances at Adam. "You were inside."

"By the door and online with her audio," Adam replies easily. "I knew when I was needed."

31

"And yet the guy got in the bathroom behind her?" Martin challenges, and he doesn't give him time for a rebuttal. He's already eyeing Blake again, challenging him now. "And what did you find behind the fence?"

"Not a damn thing," Blake replies dryly, his attention shifting to Adam. "Where is Logan right now?"

"On his way to the hospital. Savage went along for the ride, just to keep him safe."

More like make him talk, I think.

Officer Martin shifts his stance to face me more fully again. "Why were you meeting with your ex tonight?"

The "ex" comment is back again. I don't like it. "I wasn't here to meet Logan. I was here to see my parents." Which leads me to a realization. I turn to Blake. "My parents."

"Are fine," he states. "They're at home and safe. And no, I don't know if they sent Logan here tonight. Call them. We need the whole story. We don't have it without their side of this."

"I'll call them," Officer Martin interjects. "Tell me what happened in that bathroom."

"He wanted me to drop the Waters case and get back together with him," I state simply. "He said I'd be protecting him and me, as well as my family. I refused. That refusal set him off. And do you know *why* I refused his demands, Officer Martin?"

His eyes narrow but I don't give him time to reply before I add, "Because I'm the one Waters can't scare off. I'm the one who will make him rot in hell. Feel free to write that down and circulate it for review."

His eyes burn into mine and when we might have a confrontation, his cellphone rings. His lips purse and he cuts his stare, answering the call with a formal greeting of, "Officer Martin," before listening to whoever is on the other line for a few seconds. He eyes me, making it clear that the conversation is about me before he replies to his caller with, "Understood." He disconnects, his eyes on me. "Are you going to press charges?"

"I'm not in a state of mind to make that decision right now."

He surprises me by asking, "And you say you shot your ex in the foot?"

Since I've already stated this, this feels like a trick question. "Yes," I say, offering nothing more that can be used against me later.

"Interesting," he states.

Blake interjects. "What does that mean exactly?"

Officer Martin replies with his attention on me. "Your ex says he accidentally shot himself in the foot." He doesn't give me time to respond. "Tell me again where Adrian Mack is?"

"I don't know," I say. "And I hope it stays that way right up until the day he shows up in court and testifies against Waters." And because I want to be certain he knows that I know who, and what, he is, I add, "Anyone could be dirty, working for Waters, and waiting for a moment to kill Adrian," I pause for effect and add, "Even you."

Blake steps between me and Officer Martin.

Obviously, he'd sensed the explosion about to happen and he's trying to defuse it and me, but I'm not easily defused right about now. I thought I'd escaped a world where everyone bent the law to help the criminals when I'd left my father's world. Now it seems that I cannot escape. Waters' control is everywhere.

Adam steps to my side, catching my elbow and turning me to face him. "There's buzz on the dark web about Waters' hitlist, with an extra premium on you and Adrian. We need you out of here and on a plane."

I try not to process the implications of the hitlist. I mean, it's not like I don't already know how much Waters wants us all dead. But there is a dark edge to Adam I've never experienced with him, an ominous feeling to this moment that rocks me to my core. "Is Adrian okay?" I ask.

A black sedan pulls up just outside the line of police cars. "Let's go now," Adam murmurs, and he literally captures my arm and leads me toward the vehicle. Remarkably no one stops us, which I assume has something to with Blake.

Once we've reached the vehicle and Adam opens the door for me, some part of me prays Adrian is inside when I know that's not possible. We're too close to the police. I'm ushered inside and the door is shut behind me. Adrian's not here and a man I don't know is behind the wheel. Adam climbs in the front with him and we're already speeding away.

It's then that I realize Adam didn't answer my question.

Is Adrian okay?

Chapter Seven

PRI

I'm on a hitlist.

Adrian isn't here.

I'm escaping a crime scene without him, in a black sedan with some stranger behind the wheel and Adam in the passenger seat. I don't know if that makes me a criminal or what at this point and I don't even care. There is only one thing on my mind: Adrian. I lean forward in between the seats where the unknown driver and Adam share the front view.

They glance at each other, not at me, almost as if they're anticipating my question about Adrian. So much so that the dread and avoidance between them are palpable and my heart lurches with the certainty. "Tell me," I order. "Tell me what's going on with Adrian."

Adam angles toward me, lowering his voice. "He's off-mic right now, but he knows where to go and what to do."

"*Off-mic?*" I demand, and my voice isn't low at all. "Is he supposed to be off-mic? What does that mean?"

"He's riding hot," the new man states. "He's taking all precautions to ensure he doesn't get picked up by the wrong people."

"Who are *you*?" I demand. "And what does 'riding hot' mean?" I demand, because yes, I can guess, but right now, I need facts. Just facts.

"Name's Beckham," he replies. "And 'riding hot' means—"

"He's being careful," Adam supplies quickly, all too politically correct.

"Hot means trouble," I say. "He's *running* hot. I'm not a fool. He's silent because he's staying off the radar or he's already dead."

"He's not dead," snaps the new guy. "He's not dead."

I glance at him. "What do you know of it?" I don't give him time to reply. I don't know him. Adrian has never mentioned him. I face Adam. "You don't know where he is right now." And with that statement of fact, frustrated and scared for Adrian, I settle back in my seat, not sure where we're going and I don't even care. The idea of losing Adrian when I've only just found him terrifies me. And it hurts. God, the idea of losing him hurts so much.

Adam twists around to look at me. "He's smart. He didn't stay alive inside the Devils for all that time by being anything but smart."

The confirmation that I'm right about what's happening with Adrian claws at me, but I also appreciate the fact that Adam's no longer coddling me. "I know," I agree simply, a reply that comes without hesitation. Adrian *is* smart, and a survivor. The problem is that so is Waters, a man who seems to have one hand in hell and one hand right here on earth with the devil shooting the middle finger at us all.

Adam studies me a moment and apparently decides less is more in this conversation—which is accurate— and settles back into his seat. Already my mind has moved on, or rather back to the entire reason I was at that restaurant. We were leaving tonight, going underground until the trial. "We" meaning me and Adrian, with a Walker Security entourage. I'd wanted my parents to do the same. And regardless of what just took place, I still do. They're still my parents and I don't believe they expected Logan to attack me. Which is a whole other situation that weighs heavily on me, but I force that hell into a box.

I don't have time to be traumatized or rattled.

Not now.

Maybe not ever.

I need to talk to my parents, and I'm just about to inch forward to say as much to Adam when the sedan cuts right fast and sharply. I grab onto the seat and already we're turning left again. Adrenaline surges and I slide to the door to grab hold anywhere I can, as we continue a series of rapid turns, in between which we accelerate. I don't ask if we're being followed. I can only assume we are and the last thing those men in the front seat need right now are questions.

I just hold on.

A full five minutes later, we're pulling into a parking garage and I have a sense of calmer energy that has me scooting forward. "What just happened and what are we doing?"

"Changing vehicles," Adam says, offering nothing more before he opens his door and then exits. Ten seconds later, he's opening mine as well.

I climb out easily, with no purse or bag of any kind, and say, "Were we being followed?"

"We weren't taking any chances before we stopped," Adam informs me as Beckham opens the rear door to a blue SUV parked right next to us, and motions me forward.

I ignore him and focus on Adam. "I need to see my parents. I have to try to get them to listen to reason before we leave town."

Adam's jaw sets hard. "They didn't show up to your meeting. We can't trust them."

"I know that," I assure him. "I know I can't trust them, we can't trust them, but they're still my parents. I have to try."

His lips press together. "Do it by phone. For their protection and yours." He motions to the car. "Hop in."

"I don't have a phone to call them."

He reaches into his pocket and hands me one. "It's a safe line. I'll tell you when to make the call. We'll drive in circles while you make it. Throw the phone out the window when you're done."

"And then we're going to the airport?"

"Yes."

"And Adrian?"

"He'll be there," he states.

"And if he's not?" I ask, both afraid and desperate for his reply.

"He'll meet us at the safe house."

In other words, he's not sure Adrian will really make the plane. I'm not sure I can get on a plane without Adrian but I don't say that. I'll deal with that decision when the time comes. "Which is where?" I ask, fact-gathering because it makes me feel in control.

"New York," he states.

"That's Walker's headquarters. Won't Waters expect that?"

"If he does his research, he'll know how prepared we are there. If he doesn't do his research, he'll be dead."

Dead.

That's the word I hear.

"I have never wished someone dead," I say, "but I believe the world would be a better place without Waters." I don't wait for a reply. I claim my spot in the backseat of the car.

Adam seals me inside.

I glance down at the phone and I know Adam told me to wait to use the phone, but I'm freaking out about Adrian's safety. I can't help it. I dial his number. The call goes straight to voicemail.

I tell myself that means nothing.

Chapter Eight

PRI

By the time I've ended the connection with Adrian's voicemail, both of my escorts have climbed into the front of the car, with Beckham, whoever the heck he is, behind the wheel again. "I used the phone," I say. "I tried to call Adrian. Did I screw up?"

Almost instantly we're moving, and it's right as we pull out of the garage that Adam glances back at me and says, "Did he answer?"

"No. No he didn't."

"He's fine, Pri," he says quickly. "Adrian's resourceful. Hurry up and call your parents so we can dump the phone."

"Walker Security is still protecting them, right? That hasn't changed?"

"Yes," he says. "But we're doing it for you, not them. A team will pick them up. Just get them to agree."

For me.

He means for Adrian, and I'm okay with that. Adrian has a family that fell apart and in a quite tragic way. Walker has become his new family. And so have I. He just doesn't know that yet.

Now, for my family, if I can call them that.

I dial my father, the real decision-maker in our family over my mother, which was quite clear when she no-showed to dinner and didn't even warn me. My father answers on the first ring. "Who am I speaking with?"

"It's Pri."

"Pri," he greets stiffly and right there, in the coldness of his voice, I know with certainty that he sent Logan to that restaurant tonight. What I don't know is why. "What is this number you're calling from?"

I ignore the question. "You didn't show up for dinner," I say, stating the obvious.

"I thought Logan was the better choice to talk sense into you. We're not exactly on the same wavelength."

Despite the accuracy of his words, there's an undeniable twist in my gut with his statement and I hate that it exists. How can there not be, really? There was a time when he was my hero, but there's a moral separation between me and my father that continues to grow wider. On that, I grow clearer every day. And with that clarity, my hopes that he'd been blackmailed into supporting Waters' cause now seem quite ridiculous. "Have you talked to Logan?" I ask, feeling him out, for exactly what he knows or does not know. "I have not. I assume you're about to update me."

"He tried to rape me in the bathroom of my favorite Italian spot, the one I wanted to share with you and Mom this very evening. I, in turn, shot him in the foot. No one can say you didn't raise a fighter." My mind flashes back to the encounter with Logan in a small bathroom at a party two years ago now. "In hindsight, he often tried to take what wasn't his to take. And before you reply, if you'd like to justify his actions the way you did him bending his secretary over his desk while engaged to me, please do so and get it over with now."

He's dead silent. The kind of silence I've never heard from my father. Then, he says, "Can you come here to talk to me?"

"No, Father. I cannot come there to talk to you. Listen, and listen carefully. I'm on a hitlist with a large sum on my head. I'm going underground. And if you think no matter how well you serve the devil that the devil won't kill you to get to me, you're a fool. Hide. Go underground. Take Mom. If you both choose to stay, that's on you."

"You think I'm working with Waters?"

I think of the man Walker had seen on my father's security footage before showing him to me. The man who was also at the restaurant tonight and it reeks in all kinds of ways, I won't even allow my mind to travel there fully right now. "Yes. I do. If you're not, prove it."

"I don't have to prove anything," he states. "I'm not working with Waters."

"Then why send Logan to talk to me tonight?" I challenge.

"That case is causing conflict with some of the firm's clients," he states. "That topic needed to be addressed and done so in an all-business context, but I'll just say it myself. You need to step back from this case."

I blink with the realization that he's honed in on his business and only his business. "Did you hear the part where there's a hit on my head?"

"Drop the case and the hit will go away," he states almost matter-of-factly.

"Spoken with such confidence," I say, "that it's almost as if you have insider knowledge."

"I have common sense," he states. "I thought you did as well."

I ignore the jab. He's good at taking jabs. "Logan's connected to Waters. That means you are as well. I hope you've insulated yourself. Because that insulation could be the difference between you living in your mansion or inside a prison. Or even life or death."

"Drop the case," he snaps.

"I'm sending a security team to pick you and Mom up. If you choose to stay rather than go with them, either of you, that's your own bad decision. Make a good decision for once, Father, and if not for yourself, for Mom." I hang up the phone and dial my mother. She doesn't answer. I leave a message. "If you want to live, you go with the security team I'm sending to the house. Do not listen to what Dad tells you. Please be smart." I hang up and Beckham rolls down the window next to me, clearly aware of every word of my conversation.

I dial Adrian and once again, I'm thrown into his voicemail. That's when I toss the phone out of the window. Beckham rolls it up and when Adam glances back at me, I say, "Sorry for committing you like that."

"I've already got a team on the way," he assures me. "You have nothing to be sorry for. *Nothing.*"

His words radiate with sincerity. It's true that yes, he's here for me *for Adrian*, but I believe I've also built a bond with these men. I respect them. They are my friends. Adam is my friend. This is why I add, "I need you to know, and you have a right to know, that I don't think my father was blackmailed. I think he's involved with Waters and if that changes things—"

"It's doesn't," he says. "The closer he is to us, the more we control how much further he falls."

"He won't accept our protection," I say, "but maybe my mother will." But even as I speak that hopeful statement, I know she won't. There's no hope there, so

I turn to where I still have some, and ask, "Anything from Adrian?"

His lips press together again, and he offers a tightly spoken, "Not yet." He hands me another phone. "That one has your calls forwarded to it but don't be surprised if we trade it out again."

Rather than ask the millions of questions I have about what's going on back at the restaurant and with the police and Logan, I accept the phone and sink back into the leather of the seat. I can't think right now. Or rather, I can't think of anything but Adrian, right now. And so, I do. I think of him, and I replay what happened tonight. We, he and I, hand in hand, had exited that restaurant and the police had shown up instantly, not at the front of the building, but the rear. It was a setup. We walked into a trap. And Adrian was the tiger being trapped in a cage.

But they couldn't have known we'd go out the back door. Unless somehow, they did.

What was waiting for him on the other side of that fence?

Chapter Nine

PRI

Adrian *is* a tiger, a beast that is furious in battle. I saw that when he fought Deleon. And he *will* bite off the hand that taunts him. I repeat this in my head over and over during the ride to the airport, and until the car halts on a private runway next to a private plane. Adam exits the car and opens my door for me. I slide out and look at him. "Is he here?"

"Not yet," he states, and I can almost feel ice encasing my heart which will surely shatter any moment.

"We have your bags on the plane," he says. "There's food and plenty of booze, too."

Booze.

He thinks I'm going to need booze.

He thinks Adrian isn't going to show up.

"I can't leave without him."

His jaw and eyes harden in one instant. "If I don't get you on that plane, he'll find me and kill me. You mean that much to him. You get that, right?"

I press my hand to my face and knots clench my belly, emotions swelling in my chest. Adam catches my hand and pulls it from my face. "This is what he wants," he says. "You with us and safe. He'll find you and us.

47

Do this for him. And stop deciding he's dead. No more of that bullshit. None of us need that. Ever."

I inhale and breathe out, accepting the comfort and chiding in the same deserved instant. "He's not dead," I say. "He'll find us."

"He'll find *you*," he says, and he turns me to the plane. "Get on the plane, Pri."

I hurry forward and do just that. I get onto the plane. Don't ask me why, when Adam already told me Adrian isn't on board, that I hold my breath, but I do so and do so expectantly. When I round the corner to the fancy leather seats mixed up with lounge areas, a rush of disappointment overtakes me. No one is on the plane at all but me.

I don't know what that means, but I hurry to the rear of the plane where I'll be able to be alone—I hope—and where I can see who boards the plane. Choosing an area with a cluster of recliners, I sit down, my fingers digging into the leather. Dread fills me and I can't beat it back. Adam might not know what happened to Adrian, but Blake or Savage, or even Lucifer, might. Any moment, any one of them could enter the plane and deliver bad news.

That moment comes now. Male voices lift as Savage appears in the walkway, so big the plane is dwarfed with his presence. He laughs at something someone says to him and then his eyes land on me and he's abruptly serious. I'm not sure Savage is ever serious. The knots in my belly are back as he closes the space between me and him and claims a seat across from me.

"Nice shot, chickadee," he states. "I'm impressed. Smart move. Shooting that asshole in the foot."

"Adrian said losing a toe freaks a man out."

"Almost as much as losing his man candy."

48

I hold up a hand. "Please do not explain that statement. I get it."

He grins but sobers quickly, studying me with an intelligent eye. "You okay?"

"Is Adrian okay?" I counter.

"I hate bullshit. Bullshit sucks. I'm not a bullshitter. Honest answer: I don't know. He's gone silent."

There's a pinch in my belly. "It's not the answer I want," I say. "but bullshit-free is preferred, so thank you." And because I need to stay sane, I keep talking, shifting the topic. "How did you guys get me away from the police?"

"Blake pressured your boss to pull strings. Blake's more convincing than the naked eye might expose."

No doubt, I think. "What happened with Logan?"

"He's fine. I saved the dipshit's life, against my better judgment, and only to make your life simpler."

"He told them he shot himself."

His lips quirk. "Did he now?"

"You made that happen, didn't you?"

The new guy, Beckham appears beside us. "Nice shooting there, Ms. Pri Miller. I'm sure as fuck not going to mess with you."

"Buckle up!"

The shout comes from Blake. Beckham sits down next to Savage. Obviously, my plan to be alone is not working. About sixty seconds later, Adam is in the seat next to me. Blake and several other men are all huddled together up front. In what feels like a rapid progression, the doors are sealed and the engines roar to life. Adrian isn't here. He's not going to make this flight. I feel a need to throw up. I need off the plane. I reach for my belt. Adam captures my hand. "He wants you on this plane. Do this for him."

I'm breathing fast—I can't seem to control my breathing. The plane starts to taxi and I pull my hand from his. It's too late to get off. It's too late. I should not be on this plane. I lay my head back, letting the pillowed cushion offer much-needed support, letting the squeeze of my eyes hide my emotions from those watching. Instantly, I'm back at the restaurant, remembering Adrian's mouth on my mouth just before he went over that fence. I was trying to save him, not kill him.

And now—he's dead.

I know he's dead.

The plane halts abruptly and I assume it's waiting to taxi, but then there's a commotion up front. I force myself to remain calm. We wouldn't stop the plane to allow Waters' assassins into the cabin. The door is thrust open. The swish of wind is furious. That's it. I need answers. I unhook my belt, scooting forward and twisting to confront Adam. "What is happening?"

"I don't know," Adam states, unbuckling. "Stay here." He leans into the aisle and when he stands up, he doesn't go forward, but rather to the other side of the plane. What is happening? I scoot over to his seat and lean into the aisle. That's when my heart all but explodes with joy. Adrian is walking toward me. I'm on my feet in two seconds flat, running toward him.

We come together hard and fast and when his arms wrap around me and mine around him, I can finally breathe again. I didn't even know how much I needed to breathe until right now, this moment. He cups my face and kisses me, a long, deep, who-gives-a-damn-who-is-watching kiss before he says, "What the fuck were you thinking, woman?"

I don't hold back, I don't mince words or emotions. I'm all-in with Adrian. So very all-in. "I was thinking,"

I say, "that I love you too much to see you end up in jail and dead."

He breathes out and presses his forehead to mine. "That's a mistake, Pri," he whispers, and the words cut me. I'm all out there, I'm all-in, and he tells me it's a mistake?

Pain spikes in my heart with the unexpected response. We were together. We were done with obstacles. And now this. I lean back to study his face, to question him, but that action is never fully realized.

The engines roar to life, and Adrian is kissing me again, stealing my questions and objections with his skilled tongue. And when our lips part, he pulls me into a nook of two connected private seats.

I'm bothered by the confusing messages he's just delivered, by the push and pull of our passion, but the plane is flying down the runway, ready to lift off at any moment. I quickly settle into a window seat, with Adrian protectively to my left, as we both buckle up, and just in time. The plane is lifting off. Walker Security has wasted no time getting us out of Texas and I'm reminded of the hitlist.

Waters wants to kill us.

And it seems that he's managed to corrupt everyone in my life that isn't on this plane right now.

Chapter Ten

ADRIAN

Tonight was a reality check.

When I walked onto the plane, I was of the mind that Pri and I have to face the facts and deal with them accordingly. I'm touched by the devil. He will never let me go. I killed my brother. I will never be able to escape that fact. Waters will hunt me down. If Pri's with me, he'll hunt her down. Thus why my moral obligation to protect Pri has to come before my desire to be with Pri.

I knew all of this.

I knew it well.

I still know.

And then she touched me. Then she'd flung her arms around me, and I was in heaven, not hell. I didn't want to let her go.

I *don't* want to let her go. But what I want doesn't matter when it comes to saving her life.

The plane climbs through choppy air, jolting us right and left. Pri grabs my hand and I hold onto her when of course, that's the wrong move. She turns to face me and the shaking of a hot pocket of air throws her forward, and her hand lands on my leg. I feel that touch like a hot wash of heat through my body, an imprint burning through me.

She stays just like that, hand on me, dark hair in perfect disarray around her heart-shaped face, her blue eyes filled with a different kind of turbulence. "What does that mean?" she demands. "That's a mistake? I said I love you and you said that's a mistake."

I cover her hand with mine and I force myself to remember the devil's hand on my life, on my throat, choking the life out of me, the hand that might as well be on her neck. "We're on the run, living through hell together. You don't know what you'll feel when this is over." Just saying the words guts me.

Her eyes go wide, a punch of pain in their depths that guts me all over again and when she tries to pull away, I hold onto her. "Pri—"

"You're right. I got wrapped up in the heat of all of this. I just—let go."

"I don't want to let go," I say because apparently, I have no fucking self-control where she's concerned.

"I do," she whispers. "I want you to let me go."

I'm taken off guard. I'd expected her to ask me what happened. I'd expected her to want me to explain. I'd been prepared to do just that. Instead, it's almost as if she knows I'm right, and on some level, she'd make the same decision. And I fucking hate it. It takes every piece of self-control I have not to drag her to me and kiss her again. Somehow, I do what she asks, what I know is right, and I let her go.

She immediately unhooks her seatbelt and stands. I catch her hand and she jerks against my grip and tries to pass me. The plane drops hard. She gasps and buries her face in my shoulder. Holy hell, I can't let her go. I fold her closer, hold on tightly, and when the plane steadies, she lifts her face, her mouth a breath from mine. I want to kiss her. I'm going to kiss her, but she says, "No. No, I can't do this." She pushes off of me and then she's in the aisle, walking away, toward the middle of the plane.

I cover my head with my hands and curse before I lean into the aisle and watch her claim a seat far from anyone else. Squeezing my eyes shut, I lean my head back and try to think straight. Why didn't she even ask why? A million answers fly through my head. She was ready for this. She knew it had to happen. She wasn't sure she really loved me. I mean, we've only known each other for a few weeks. Or of course, there's the other option: I hurt her. And damn it, she's been hurt by everyone in her life.

PRI

Hurrying down the aisle of the plane, I move away from Adrian, and my heart is beating too fast.

My emotions are out of control. I'm really not an emotional person. I've stood across from many a monster and never even blinked. But Adrian is no monster. He's the man I'd assumed myself in love with. But he's right. We don't know what we feel right now. We've known each other for a few weeks. That means we're in lust, not love, infatuated at best. I'm infatuated with my key witness and that's trouble.

I find an open lounge area with blankets and pillows and I sit down, scolding myself as I do. I'm the lead prosecutor on a dangerous case against a dangerous man. That comes with responsibility. I owe Waters' victims my focus, my best. That means I can't be distracted by a personal relationship with a witness.

Everything that is not about this case has to be set aside.

And yet somehow, my mind flashes to a moment in the bathroom when Logan's hands had been all over me when his tongue had been in my mouth. I press my hands to my face. "I shot him," I whisper, and my eyes open and land on a little compartment under the bench across from me, where there seems to be a minibar filled with, you guessed it, mini bottles of whiskey. I'm not a drinker, but I'm thirty thousand feet in the air and I shot my ex in the foot tonight after he almost raped me. I'm certainly not going to talk about what happened, so drinking it away seems logical. Besides, even if I was going to talk about it, the one person I might have done so with is Adrian, and he's no longer on the options list as of a few minutes ago.

Adrian and I are no longer personal. That's how it has to become. That's how it has to be. He knows it. I know it.

Decision made, at least where the drink is concerned, I squat down in front of the minibar, grab a bottle, and I don't even look at what I'm about to be drinking. I open the top, and gulp it, choking with the bite of amber liquid sliding down my throat. Once I've shoved the bottle in the trashcan that is by the little bar area, I sit back down.

I grab a pillow and hold it to me, and already the numbing effect of the whiskey is overcoming me and it's sweet bliss. I lay down on the bench and unbidden, I'm back in the moment when Adrian walked onto the plane. Then the moment when my arms were around him and his were around me. And when his mouth had come down on my mouth, I'd tasted his passion, his desperation, his fear. His love. Or not.

What do I really know of love?

What do I know of anything right now? Well, aside from the fact that my father is dirty. My ex is a monster. My mother is a fool. And his conviction or not, Waters will never quit coming for me or Adrian. Not as long as he's alive. I've never wished someone dead, but I do him. Waters is the devil on earth. And I can't even believe I just had that thought.

Chapter Eleven

ADRIAN

"Move your ass over."

At Savage's gruff demand, I don't fight the command. He has something to say and he'll say it to the whole damn plane if I don't give him room to join me and say it to me. "What do you want, Savage?"

"No appreciation for the wicked, I see. I saved that asshole back there."

"And that's supposed to please me?"

"Pri doesn't have to deal with a death investigation, so yes. You should be so fucking pleased you pee yourself."

"What do you want, Savage?"

"For you to listen. You don't have to talk." He pulls a bottle of whiskey from his pocket and hands it to me. "But you can drink if you want."

On that, I don't argue. We have hours on this plane, hours with Pri somewhere other than by my side. I open the bottle and take a slug, offering it to him. He downs a drink and says, "Candace and I were engaged years ago. And apart years after. Because like a dumb-ass fucktard, I left her."

"I was there when you were trying to win her back. I know pieces of this story."

59

"I didn't trust you worth a shit back then. You know very little. Obviously not enough since you're being a fucktard yourself right now. So listen up and listen well, because my story is your story." He slugs a drink and keeps talking. "I'd been dragged into an off-the-books military operation and my reasons for getting involved were right. Where it led me was not. I became a killer. And as any self-respecting killer would, I made enemies." He hands me the bottle. "She would have been a target. And fuck, man, I left a surgeon. I would have come back an assassin."

Now it's my turn to slug back another drink and damn, I feel the burn this time in more ways than one. He's trying to give me a reason to stay with Pri and I fucking want it. But that doesn't make it right. "And now you're married."

"After years of being miserable without her. I tried to fuck her out of my system. I took jobs I was certain would get me killed. I liked that idea. I drank too much. I did all the standard miserable loser things I could do. None of it worked. And the fucked-up part? The enemy found her anyway."

I pause mid-drink and look at him. "I know this part. Someone went after her."

"Hell yeah, they went after her. And then so did I."

I'd be irritated that he was telling me what I already know, if he didn't have a point— he's trying to make me think and it's working. Would Waters keep coming for Pri? The answer is yes unless I make him believe she's my enemy, too. I don't even want to think about how I'd do that. I down another drink. "Obviously Candace forgave you."

He snorts and grabs the bottle. "But don't forget, she was engaged to another man, about to get married.

I wanted to kill that bastard. It about destroyed me. And she hated my ass."

I snort at that, remembering that well. "She really did hate your ass."

"Yeah, and that could be you with Pri." I open my mouth to speak and he holds up a hand. "Listen, don't talk. She was miserable when we were apart and so was I. She was settling for that little dick prick, forcing herself to move on. I did a lot of begging to win her back, and I'm not even afraid to admit it. She helped me crawl out of hell and find a way to be human again." He shifts his tone and eyes me. "You won't save Pri by leaving her. In fact, with a man like Waters, she's safer with you by her side—well, me by her side. You're a pussy bitch ex-FBI agent. I'll take care of her for you."

"Bastard," I mumbled.

He grins. "And you know you're starting to love me. I'm so fucking lovable."

I ignore his self-admiration, already sobering on thoughts of Pri. I grab the bottle and down another swig, the welcome numbing effect starting to kick in. "She barely knows me, Savage." I hand him the bottle.

"You mean she doesn't know what happened between you and your brother."

I scrub a hand through my hair. "Yeah. That." I sink back in the seat and I'm back in that bathroom with Logan and Pri while Logan screams, *"He's a killer. He killed his brother. And he'll fuck you to the finish and then kill you, too."*

And that can't be how this ends. Me getting Pri killed. Or if I go with Savage's version of this, me leaving her behind to end up dead. *Waters should stay in jail,* I think. I can't get to him there because if I see him again, if I get the chance to kill him again, I will.

Chapter Twelve

ADRIAN

Savage doesn't have an off button. You tell him something that would shut someone else up and he just keeps talking. And apparently, the big badass assassin is in confession mode. "Candace didn't know a lot of shit I did, either," he says. "Not when we first reconnected. But eventually, you have to tell Pri if you want the two of you to work."

He's not wrong, I think. In or out with Pri, personally, I can't hide from who I am. "Sooner than later," I say. "It's becoming a hot trial issue. Waters' defense will use it to discredit me."

"Then sooner it is," he says. "I didn't like it. You won't like spilling that dirt to Pri, man. It won't feel good. It won't be fun. But like I said, trial or no trial, if you want to make it work with her, you have to let her in, tell it all—good, bad, and ugly. You have to trust her to see that there's more to you."

"Logan told her I'm a killer," I say. "He told her I'd kill her eventually, too."

"Is that what this is about? You let that dweeb get in your head."

"I was already there."

"Look, man. I'm not a candy man. I don't sugarcoat shit. Truth be told, maybe Pri can't handle the truth, but you have to tell her anyway. And truth be told, maybe it's not the right time. Maybe she has a hero complex right now for you. Make sure it's real before you tell her. I don't know what is real shit or not for you two, but hear this and hear it well. Don't assume walking away from her is the best way to love her. That's you fucking up. And on that devastatingly brilliant note, I have to take a piss." He hands me the bottle, stands up, and disappears.

My mind is replaying this night again. Pri's parents betrayed her. Logan betrayed her. And then I did the same. I set the bottle down and get up, wasting no time finding Pri. She's laying down in a lounge area now, a blanket pulled over her. My heart swells just looking at her. If that doesn't mean I'm in love, I don't know what does.

I stand there a minute, just looking at her, afraid of waking her up, but she must sense I'm there. Suddenly she jerks up, spies me, and sits up. Then she's staring at me. And I'm staring at her. And what I see in her eyes is pain hidden behind bravado. Pain I want to erase. I slide down beside her and she holds up a hand. "Adrian—"

My mouth closes down on hers. She resists, at least she holds back, her body stiff, but when my tongue meets hers, she moans and softens in my arms.

For the moment, she's mine again. And I want that moment to last. Our lips part and I say, "We'll talk later, really talk. But I need you to be okay with that, baby, because I've been drinking, but the idea of you up here and me back there, I don't like it. And Pri, I'm—"

"I don't like it either," she whispers, her fingers curling on my jaw. "Later is okay."

WHEN HE'S WILD

I kiss her again, wild, passionate, out of control when we can't be out of control on the plane, not with all the company we have. I lay down with her, behind her, and wrap myself around her. I do exactly what I told myself before I got on this plane that I shouldn't do. I hold onto her.

Chapter Thirteen

ADRIAN

I lay there holding Pri as the plane hums, steady and calm now, perhaps the first steady calm we've had for weeks. Pri falls asleep almost instantly and I wonder if she feels what I do, that we're above it all here, all of it, the bullshit, the danger, where we can just exist without looking over our shoulders. It also tells me that when she's with me, she feels safe.

She feels safe.

Despite Logan screaming about me killing her.

I hold her a little tighter and shut my eyes, and I'm instantly drifting into that haze of near slumber with my mind not quite willing to let me rest. Suddenly it seems I'm in the past, sitting at a bar table with Waters in between me and Deleon. It was the first time we were the pack of three we became.

"I need her," Waters says, *motioning to the woman in the red dress at the bar.*

Unease rolls through me, but I play it cool. "I doubt her boyfriend will agree," I comment dryly, sipping my beer. The boyfriend in question is a good six feet plus, muscular, with tats, but he's no King. He doesn't stand a chance with Waters.

Waters is watching her, stroking his beard, a recent addition to a face he's found in the press as of late after a missing woman was connected to him.

The boyfriend, or whoever the guy is with the woman, eyes Waters, and fuck, he's got attitude. Waters wiggles his tongue at the woman, whose eyes go wide. Deleon laughs as the man puffs up and charges toward us. Deleon stands up and meets him in the middle. The next thing I know, Deleon grabs him and starts dragging him toward the door.

The woman stands up, screaming for help, completely freaked out. But there is no help in a bar packed with Devils. She and her man stumbled into the wrong place at the wrong time. She runs for the door.

Waters smirks and eyes me. "Go get her for me," *Waters orders.*

I sip my beer and laugh. "If you want someone to help you dip your cock, man, you got the wrong guy." *I down the rest of my drink and stand up.* "I'm going to take a piss." *I head for the back of the bar, hoping like hell my gamble pays off and convinces Waters I'm not a fed. I'm the cocky-ass right-hand man he needs.*

The woman screams, and my fingers curl into my palms. I can't fucking help her. There's nothing I can do. I walk into the bathroom, and shut the door, pressing my hand to the surface. I can't let that woman end up in the next missing bulletin. I can't do it. I grab my phone and shoot a text to Kirk Pitt, another agent working the Water's case but from afar: Get a patrol to Longhorn Bar off county road 1220. And just in case, send an ambulance. And get tech to wipe this message. *I delete the message, take a piss, and hope like hell for the best as I return to the bar.*

Not a single member of the Kings is left in the bar.
They left.
I eye the bartender. "Where the fuck did they go?"
"I told them I called the cops," he says. "They took
off. Why don't you get smart and do the same?"
My lips press together and I eye the barstools
where the woman in the red dress and her boyfriend
had been sitting. "What happened to the couple?"
"She followed them outside, trying to find her
boyfriend. So what the hell do you think happened?"
I curse and run for the door. Sirens sound in the
distance as I exit and find the boyfriend laying in the
center of the parking lot. I rush to his side, and squat
down, checking for a pulse. It's weak but it's there. An
ambulance turns into the far-right entrance. Help has
arrived for the man, but I'm the only hope that woman
has. I leave the man where he lies, run to my bike, and
climb on, not sure how I save her and not get us both
killed. But I have to try.

I blink awake, instantly aware of Pri's backside
pressed close, while Blake stands above us. Pri must
sense his presence as well, as she gasps and sits up. I go
with her and then we're side by side as the plane jolts.

"Bumpy landing expected," Blake says. "You two
need to buckle into a seat."

"I have to go to the bathroom first," Pri says,
standing and hurrying past Blake.

He hands me a bag. "Chick-fil-A. Somehow
Beckham managed to grab us enough to feed an army
before takeoff. I heated it up for you. And in case you
don't already know, that was a fucked-up decision you
made tonight, going into that restaurant."

"Are you telling me you wouldn't have made it for
your wife?"

"Pri isn't your wife."

"Are you telling me you wouldn't have done it before you married Kara?"

"Are you telling me you're going to marry Pri?" he counters.

The question explodes in my mind, taunting me with everything I am and once was, everything I can't be for Pri. Everything I wish I could be for Pri. "I'm telling you that her safety comes before mine. And that isn't going to change."

Suddenly Pri is standing next to Blake. "I don't want to be alive and miserable because you're dead, Adrian. You shouldn't have been in that restaurant tonight. The end." She glances at Blake. "Please tell me that food is for us."

"It is," Blake says, handing her the bag. "Chick-fil-A compliments of Beckham."

The plane jolts and instantly Blake and I steady our feet, and each of us presses a hand to the ceiling for support. A moment later, I grab Pri and pull her to me. Blake's eyes meet mine and his lips quirk. "There's a reason you put on your own oxygen mask before you save the person next to you. The premise is one we both know well. We both understand we can't protect those we love if we're dead."

In other words, that's exactly, instinctually, what I just did.

He steps around us and walks down the aisle.

Chapter Fourteen

ADRIAN

The plane stabilizes, at least for the moment, and I urge Pri to take advantage of the stable ground. "Let's get buckled in," I say, taking the bag of food from her to allow her to move down the aisle ahead of me with free hands to grab for stability if needed. Once she's in her earlier seat, I set the bag of food down in mine. "I'll get us drinks."

She lifts the whiskey bottle. "We have this."

I glance at the all but empty bottle. "I think it's time for some water."

She smiles and slugs back some whiskey before coughing and hoarsely agrees, "Yes. Please. Water."

Pri doesn't grab a bottle and drink. She's too much of a control freak, but she's making such a cute face that now I'm doing the impossible, and smiling, because that's what Pri does for me. She drags me from the swampland where I'm drowning in criminal slime and self-hate, and I see light again, at least for a moment. The problem is that once you're in the swampland, you're forever marked. I'm marked. And apparently, I'm trying like hell to mark her, too.

I turn away from her and walk to one of several mini-fridges in the plane, grab two waters, and when the plane begins to shudder, I'm reminded of a smooth flight turned bumpy years back. The flight attendant ended up smacking the ceiling and being slammed to the ground. I'd stabilized her broken leg and handed her four bottles of whiskey to get her to the ground. There's a lesson in that memory, and that lesson is to never, ever forget that the calm is always before the storm. Pri is the calm. Waters is the storm. And this doesn't end until he's dead. And the bastard's father lived to a hundred and one.

I head back to my seat and settle in next to Pri, placing the waters in the drink holders. She hands me a sandwich. "Don't worry," she says. "There's more where that came from. They gave us four. I'm only eating one."

I don't argue. I'm still all about replacing the whiskey in my body with something else and making sure I'm whole again when we set down in New York. I open my wrapper and for a few moments that stretch into about two minutes, we both eat. It's a comfortable silence despite the heat and conflict between us. There are things I could say to Pri, and things she could say to me, no doubt, questions she could ask, and probably burns to ask, but I think we both know that we need to be alone for that conversation, and not on a clock.

Which is a real thing.

Judging from the downward trajectory of the plane, we'll be on the ground in twenty minutes, and it will be time for me to make a decision: Let Pri go to the Walker building, where the Walker family will keep her safe. Or take her home with me. I want her to go home with me, but it feels like a turning point. Once she's there, once she's in my home, there's no turning back.

I finish off my sandwich and Pri hands me another. When we're done eating, and our altitude is quickly decreasing, Pri turns to face me. "Thank you for being worried about me tonight."

"Thank you?" I challenge softly. "I don't need a thank you, Pri."

"I know," she says quickly. "I get that. You did it because you were worried."

"Losing my fucking mind worried," I amend.

"Then you know how I felt when you went over that fence and I feared it was a trap."

It was, I think, but I don't tell her that now. Not when she clearly has a point to make. Not when we're so close to an abrupt ending to any conversation that starts now. "You don't have to be with me, Adrian. There's no obligation here because of who I am and who you are."

"There was never an obligation to us, Pri."

"As you said—"

"That was—"

"Complicated," she says. "*I know*." And then to my surprise, she says nothing else. She settles back in her seat and grips the arms, her fingers digging deep into the leather. Whatever she'd been about to say, she's decided against.

And I'm not sure what to think about that.

Chapter Fifteen

PRI

Once Adrian and I are on the ground, reality slams into me. We're here because we're hiding from a madman who is alive and well and will stay that way. When does this end? *How* does that end? And of course, I'd sworn off Adrian one minute, and I'm pretty sure he'd done the same with me, but the next moment, we were kissing, and then falling asleep in each other's arms. He could have died tonight protecting me. We are not good for each other and yet it's as if we're both drugged when we're together.

We're a mess.

Waters wins when we're a mess.

Once we've deplaned into the bitter cold of New York City, I'm instantly wishing for a winter coat. Adrian shrugs out of his light leather jacket and folds it around my shoulders. "We'll get you a coat tomorrow," he promises, a promise that assumes we'll be together tomorrow. He also carries my bag that was packed in advance and his hand, warm despite the cold night, rests possessively under the jacket on my lower back as I climb in the back of an SUV. We're not doing a good job of being professional, but then I guess he never said we needed to be professional. That was my thought. He simply said we're not in love, or something close enough, to have me down a bottle of whiskey. A mini bottle, but to me, that's plenty big enough for an impact.

I'm not sure where any of that leaves us or leads us for that matter.

Once we're sealed in the vehicle, with the heat cranked nice and warm, the driver turns to greet me. Even before he says, "Hi, Pri. I'm Luke Walker. It's nice to meet you," I've recognized his familiar dark good looks.

"Hi, Luke," I say, "You look like your brothers," I say, having spent plenty of time with Blake, and having met Royce on video chat when he and Lauren were in Chicago trying to get the warrant for Adrian's arrest dropped.

"So I hear," he says. "But I'm the reasonable one. And the nice one. Which is why I'm going to get you to a bed without delay or challenge." He glances at his watch. "It's after midnight. We can all get together and talk about Waters tomorrow."

He settles back in his seat and sets us in motion. Adrian scoots closer to me and his hand comes down on my knee, branding me, and he holds me close. He's not even pretending we broke up or we're stepping away from each other. I try to think back to what happened on the plane and the truth is he never said that's what he wanted. He just said that loving him was a mistake. And I'm pretty sure him worrying about me to the point he puts himself at risk is a mistake.

We turn onto the main road and it hits me that this is where Adrian lives. Am I going to his apartment? Will I see his home? Or not. Nerves erupt in my belly. As far as I'm concerned, our destination tells me where his head is right now.

A few minutes later, I find out my answer. We pull up to the Ritz Carlton Hotel.

I'm not going to Adrian's apartment. I'm not going to his home. Of course, there could be other reasons for this decision, but right now, there's no question the hotel location stings.

There's also a ball in my chest, a tight ball, but I tell myself this is for the best. The only man in my life right now needs to be Waters, and I have to find a way to shut him down, really shut him down. The vehicle halts and Luke exits the vehicle. Adrian opens his door and exits as well, leaning in to tell me, "Hold tight a moment."

He doesn't wait for a reply. He shuts me back inside and I'm suddenly suffocating in the heat blowing from the vents. I shut one and the door opens again, blasting me with cold air. Adrian, now wearing another jacket, which I assume is meant to cover up the weapon at his side, offers me his hand and just the idea of touching him right now turns me hot all over again. I tug Adrian's jacket around me and slide out of the back seat, and the minute I'm outside, I'm aware of Savage and Adam's presence. Adrian pulls me under his arm and walks me toward the lobby, sheltering me—he's always sheltering me, no matter what the cost. And there is a cost. Maybe he doesn't love me but this man could have died for me tonight.

I'm not good for him. He gets that. I know he does. We both know. And it's time for us both to do what is right. And what is right is me stepping back from Adrian. He can't risk his life for me and he will if we don't cut out the personal. That realization alone makes the hotel suddenly the right choice. He has to live. Nothing else matters. And yet I don't pull away from Adrian. God, the idea of not touching him, not being with him, affects me like nothing else has. Yes, it

77

hurt when Logan cheated, but I've long ago decided that was about the entire façade of my life falling apart. Not him. Not me with him.

Savage and Adam fall into place at either side of us and somehow these men feel like my family too, when my own family does not. And yet, they aren't my family, I remind myself. Still how insane is it that I believe that any one of these men would come through for me in ways my family would not. A realization that is both good and painful. There's been a lot happening these past few days. I'm not sure how I feel about any of it.

Once we're on the elevator, the four of us, Adam punches our floor, and the doors shut. Adrian tugs me in front of him, my back to his front, his hand possessively at my waist as if he thinks I'll escape. I don't want to escape. I want us to be two normal people that can be together. No. Normal is overrated. I don't want to be normal. I want to win against Waters.

For now, that lack of control Waters has delivered unto us has me ticking off the floors, wanting out of this small car. No, I'm not exactly claustrophobic right now, and elevators don't seem to be triggers, but I'm suffocating in everything, just everything, right now. I need air. I need space.

The car opens and when I would step forward, Savage holds out a hand in front of me to stop me. He moves ahead of me, searches the hallway, and then motions for us to follow.

The very fact that Savage had to clear our path drives home every reason we're in this hotel, on the run, and all those reasons lead back to Waters. I step back into the hallway and Adrian's arm is already on me. They're all too protective and I'm suddenly reminded of what Adam told me back in Austin. There's a hit out on me and Adrian, a *high-priced* hit on each of us, and that hit has them all on edge. They chose to come to New York, but they brought me here, to a hotel. Suddenly that decision doesn't feel like it's about me and Adrian. It feels like it's about Waters. It feels like it's about an active threat to our lives that may have escalated even further.

Chapter Sixteen

PRI

We reach the end of the hallway and Adrian uses a keycard to open a door. Without a word, Adam and Savage go left and right to separate doors. They're staying here as well. And yet, they live here in New York. *I think.* I'm almost certain. Adrian motions me into the room. I enter the fancy room with a living area, and move forward quickly, feeling some odd fight or flight mechanism that shows itself as flight. I'm not sure who I'm running from. Waters? Myself? Adrian?

I step beyond the living area, and behind the couch that faces the foyer. When Adrian emerges from said foyer and enters the room, my fingers curl on the leather back of the couch.

He halts at the line of the living room. "What are you doing, Pri?"

"Don't Savage and Adam live here in New York City?"

"They do."

"Don't you live here, Adrian?"

"I do."

"What is going on?" I press.

He moves then, rounding the couch, and I turn to face him. He stops a few steps from me—no, a long

81

stride from me—but seems to hesitate. All that drama on the plane between us has now landed right here, in this room. "We're just being cautious," he says. "We need to know no one followed us."

"Do we think we were followed?" I ask, wanting to know exactly where we stand.

"We're being cautious, Pri," he reiterates, in what one might say is avoidance.

"I know we're on a hitlist," I counter, ensuring he knows that I'm not going to be coddled or left in the dark.

"Nothing has changed," he says. "You know Waters wants anyone in his path dead."

"I know he upped the price on our heads. Adam told me."

His lips thin. "Adam talks too much."

"We're here tonight. What about tomorrow?"

"We'll see what intel says tomorrow," he replies.

I'm aware of the small space between us that is wider than it seems. And in that space stands Waters and more. Life and death. That space is, in fact, *all about* life and death and that's why neither of us has closed it. I take a step backward. "Do I have my own room?"

There's a sharpening of his mood, a slight stiffening of his spine before he questions, "Why would you need your own room, Pri?"

"The same reason you needed your own space on that plane, Adrian."

"I came back to you."

"But you knew you shouldn't have. And you were right."

A muscle in his jaw tics. "Right about what, Pri?"

"We don't know what we feel."

He steps toward me. "Pri—"

I hold up a hand and take another long step backward. "We don't know what we feel, Adrian, that much is true. We both know it's true, but I do know that what I feel for you is nothing like what I felt for Logan. *Nothing*. That's what I know. It's more intense, it's more, well, for a lack of a better word, deep and—and maybe that's about the circumstances. I don't know. But I know you got on that plane tonight, and I know that you took a risk because of me. Knowing I'm bad for you."

"*You're bad for me*? Are you crazy, woman? I got on that plane knowing that *I'm* bad for *you*. I'm bad for you. As long as you're my woman, Waters will come for you. You will never be safe because he will never let me walk away from this. It's him or me, and I missed the chance to make it him."

But he doesn't move toward me.

The space between us just seems to grow.

"So we're bad for each other," I say. "That's what we're saying. I need to go to bed. I need to rest and think and wake up tomorrow ready to fight Waters." And because I know he knows what's right, I try to make it easier on him. "I need to do that alone. That's what I *want*, Adrian."

"We both know that's not true."

"We're not good for each other," I remind him, and I mean it. We're *not* good for each other. Not now. Probably not in this lifetime.

He studies me long and hard and then there's a knock on the door. His lips press together. "That will be our bags," he says. "I'll take mine to Savage's room." And with that, he turns and walks away. And with that, despite what my words have said, my heart crashes to the ground and shatters.

I draw in a breath that seems to expand in my chest with painful force. The door opens and closes. With it, I feel that "the end" for me and Adrian has come. I can feel myself unraveling in a way I never did with Logan. When we parted ways, it was time, it was right. This doesn't feel right and yet, I'm protecting Adrian. That feels right.

I grab the couch and holding on, my fingers pressed into the cushion, I wait and wait, and then the door opens and closes again. Adrian left and now he's back. Without any ability to stop myself, I round the couch and enter the foyer to have disappointment jab at me. Adrian isn't here, but my suitcase is sitting by the door. *The end,* I think again. Riding my emotions, I grab the bag and hurry down the hallway, finding the master bedroom with a master bath attached. I'm aware that I didn't latch the door, I'm aware that's because I hope Adrian will return, but I'm not going to think about what that means about where I'm at with him. For now, I have no idea why a hot bath is my place of escape, but it is, and that premise entices me. However, I don't think I can wait on the water to run. I'm cold, so very cold, all of a sudden.

I turn on the shower and strip down as the water warms up. I step into the fancy stone-framed shower and let the hot water run over me.

The night crashes down around me. God, it crashes down. My parents' betrayal, Logan's hands all over me, Adrian and I breaking up. Waters. Waters just won't stop coming at us and I'm letting him win. New emotions crash over me, hot water trying to burn them away, and I will it to work. I need it to work. When it fails, I turn off the water, dry off, wrap my hair and then pull on the giant hotel robe. That's when unbidden, tears flow down my cheeks. I don't fight them for good reason. I know myself. I am strongest once I've been weak, but I have to allow myself to feel the wounds. And so, I do. I rest against the wall, sink down onto the floor, and the explosion comes. I quake from the inside out and I don't even try to fight it.

My face is buried in my hands, my knees to my chest when a shift in the air washes over me. My gaze jerks upward, but already Adrian is there, strong hands lifting me, and then I'm folded against his big body.

Chapter Seventeen

PRI

At this moment, with Adrian's mouth on my mouth, his hands on my body, I don't have it in me to do what I never wanted to do in the first place—*push Adrian away*. Right or wrong, tomorrow be damned, there is only now.

I inhale the masculine spice of him, sink into the hard lines of his body, melting where I stand, the towel on my head falling away. He is warm and big and strong and I'm still weak, still not beyond the emotion that this day has refused to allow me to ignore. Still so very far away from the calm, stronger me after the storm.

Adrian folds me close, one hand between my shoulder blades, the other at the back of my head. "I didn't want to leave," he declares. "I can't be without you, Pri. Why do you think I lost my mind when you were trapped in the bathroom with Logan? When that bastard followed you and I was too far away from stopping what came next."

My anger comes hard and fast, a product of hours upon hours of pent-up emotions and fear. Fear for me. Fear for my parents. Fear for Adrian. My fingers curl on his chest and my stare pierces his. "You shouldn't have come into that restaurant."

"I had to protect you."

"You didn't," I say. "I appreciate your concern. I appreciate it so much, but I had help nearby. I had my weapon. I had training. Leave me, break up with me, do whatever you need to do, but damn it, you *don't get to die on me*. Do you understand?"

"He tried to rape you, Pri." His voice is low, rough, affected, a confirmation that everyone listening to the audio knew what Logan did to me. I knew that, of course, I did. I had that conversation with the police, and yet knowing Adrian heard, that gets to me more than anything. "No decent man could hear that, Pri," he adds, "and sit back and wait for that to happen. Or count on someone else to rescue his woman."

His woman.

His need to be a decent man for me.

His fear that he can never be even close to decent. Somehow he still doesn't understand just how bad my bad was at one point.

"Adrian," I whisper. "You do know—"

"I know I'd do it again. No," he amends, "I'd stop it from happening next time. I would *stop it* from happening, Pri."

He was protecting me. He *is* protecting me. He is always protecting me and I don't let myself think about where that could lead him. Because that leads me to push him away again and I don't want him to leave. Right or wrong, now or ever. My mind skips back to that bathroom, to Logan attacking me, to the entire Walker clan hearing it happen, and my fingers twist around Adrian's shirt. "Make me forget he ever touched me. Make me forget and—"

His mouth is on my mouth once more, his tongue a sultry lick against mine. I moan with the taste of him, whiskey and man, and already he's untied my robe, his warm hands sliding under the terry cloth and over my skin. His hands are all over my body, running up and down my back, one palm scooping my backside and dragging me closer, the thick ridge of his erection pressed to my belly. "Logan will never kiss you or touch you again," Adrian vows, nipping my lip.

I gasp with the unexpected pinch, but already Adrian laves the ache with his tongue. Somehow that tiny act is a promise of protection.

I breathe out on a pant, aware I'm probably overthinking everything, too in my head. He drags me back into the moment with a kiss, a fast, seductive lick, before our lips part and his hot gaze lowers, traveling over my naked breasts. And when his gaze returns to mine, he repeats his words. "He will *never* touch you again, Pri."

And then my breasts are in his hands, his fingers on my nipples, and he's kissing me again, drugging me, and in that moment, all the cold I'd felt earlier, evaporates. It's simply gone, and there is nothing left but heat, burning hot heat. My body is on fire. My body craves him and only him. I tug at his shirt, my fingers sliding underneath the tee, my palm pressing to hot, taut skin and rippling muscle. Adrian reaches behind him and pulls the shirt over his head. Before it ever hits the ground, my hands are back on his body. I'm touching him, I just need to touch him. And for him to touch me. He cups my head and kisses me even as he slides my robe down my shoulders and pulls my naked body against him.

My breasts are heavy, my sex aching, and when the robe falls to the ground, I am naked in every possible way with Adrian. This man has the ability to hurt me in a way no other human has ever possessed. Because he possesses me. He owns me in ways I didn't know I could be owned and he doesn't even really know it. Which only makes him own me all the more.

His eyes travel my body in an erotic inspection that puckers my nipples and clenches my sex. And when his gaze lifts and meets mine, I swear I melt right here where I stand. He leans in closer, that masculine spice assaulting my senses, and he nuzzles my neck, his breath warm where it fans over my skin. Goosebumps lift on my skin and his lips press to the sensitive spot under my ear.

He murmurs something low that I can't understand and then cups my backside, lifting me from the cold tile floor. My legs wrap around his waist and then he's carrying me to the bedroom, where the lights are dim and the burn between us is hot. He lays me on the bed and then stands to undress.

I sit up, oblivious to my own nakedness as I watch him pull off his boots and then reach for his pants. A moment later, his cock juts free, thick and lightly veined, his entire body lean but muscular. He is a work of art, a man who knows excess in only one thing: self-hate. I vow in that moment to change that or at least love him more than he hates himself.

He moves toward me and as he does, I lay back. Then he is over me, his hands on either side of my head, his big body over my body. His lips find my neck, my ear, and he whispers something in Spanish. It seems he has things to say tonight that he doesn't want me to understand when I need to understand.

My fingers dive into his thick, dark hair and I'm rewarded with his mouth, his tongue, his kiss that devours me, and almost makes me forget to ask, "What did you say in Spanish?" I whisper. "What did it mean?"

He pulls back and stares down at me, seconds ticking by, the lines of his handsome face drawn tight. "One day I'll tell you," he promises finally, and then adds, "but not today."

I don't like this answer, but he kisses me, and his hands cup my breasts and I am no longer capable of thinking. There are just sensations and pleasure, so much pleasure. His mouth on my mouth, his fingers on my nipple, then his mouth that follows. And then his lips on my belly, his tongue teasing the delicate skin. His eyes meeting mine with the promise of where his mouth will go next.

And it does.

He slides lower, his shoulders between my thighs, spreading me wider, exposing me more fully to him. And then his breath is hot on my sex, his tongue teasing my clit, his mouth even hotter as he licks and teases. My fingers are in his hair, my hips lifting, my body awash in sensations, but just when I'm trembling with absolute desire, with the edge of release, he is gone. His mouth, his tongue, his fingers that had found a way inside me, stretching me, pleasing me, are gone. Moments before I might have come, he is gone.

I gasp and try to sit up, but he's already rolling us to our sides, facing each other. "Adrian," I breathe out, his name one part objection and one part plea. But then his hand on my backside, scooping me to him, the thick ridge of his erection pressed between my legs, nestled intimately against the wet heat of my sex. I'm no longer objecting. "You come with me inside you tonight," he murmurs, and then he's kissing me, the salty taste of *me* on his lips.

He whispers Spanish in my ear again and then he asks, "Do you trust me, Pri?"

My fingers curl on his jawline, the rough scruff of his stubble a rasp against my palm. "You know I do."

"For now," he says, "but I'll take what I can get from you, Pri. And now," he says, softly, "I'm going to make you forget." I'm about to object to the "for now" comment, but Adrian smacks my backside just hard enough to shock me.

I yelp with the impact and arch forward and he takes advantage of that reaction. He presses inside me, driving deep. "Think of me," he orders softly and I have this sense that he's not talking about how he replaces Logan. "Remember me," he adds, and with that I know he means later when he's gone, but before I can press him, he presses me.

Or rather his palm comes down on my backside again and he thrusts into me and then all words escape me. His mouth devours mine, his cock thrusts deep inside me and his hand comes down on my backside in random, somehow perfect, and oh so erotic moments. I lose time and space, and there is just us, me and Adrian, our bodies intimately bound, moving together. Our ragged breaths. Our desperate kisses. And we are desperate in ways that I don't believe anyone else would understand. We're alive. We don't know if we'll be alive tomorrow. And on some level, there's this sense that we're losing each other. We want each other and right now, we *need* each other.

I savor every moment of the pleasure. I don't want this to end, but my body has other ideas. Release comes over me hard and fast. I bury my head in Adrian's neck, holding onto him, my body stiff for a moment before I gasp with a spasm. He groans a low, masculine groan,

and drives deeper, harder, faster, and then we're
trembling together, bodies quaking.
  We are one.
  At least, *for now.*

Chapter Eighteen

PRI

For long moments—no, not moments, but minutes actually, I really have no concept of time—Adrian and I just hold one another. It's me who breaks the silence, me who dares to lead us into what I know may be an explosion of yet more emotions.

"What does 'for now' mean, Adrian?" I whisper.

His body stiffens and he doesn't look at me. "Let me get you a towel and the robe." He pulls out of me and rolls over and I swear the wall between us that was there on that plane for a small portion of our trip here, slams back into place. He's standing in an instant, walking toward the bathroom in all his naked perfection, snatching up his pants as he goes. but it's me who feels naked in every possible way. But I don't let myself reach for the blanket. If I want Adrian to expose all of himself to me, I have to be willing to be exposed with him. And that's what I want. That's what I've always wanted and the one thing I'm not sure will ever happen.

He hates himself. He believes I will hate him if I really know everything about him. He's wrong.

Still, I grab a tissue, clean up, and scoot up to a sitting position, knees to my chest. When Adrian exits the bathroom, he's in his jeans, holding the robe and a towel. The wall is still there between us, but space is another story. He closes what is between us and sits down in front of me. He offers me the towel and I take it and set it aside. He slides the robe around me and slips my arms into the sleeves, but before I can fully close it, his hands are behind my knees. "Don't read into what I said, Pri."

"You know the old saying," I say. "Drunk people and people about to have orgasms speak the truth."

His lips quirk, softening the hard lines of his face. "I've never heard that saying."

"Well, now you have," I point out. "You have to stop hating yourself for me."

"I'm protecting you."

"And that's exactly where the trouble starts. Stop protecting me."

"I can't do that, Pri. I'm not even going to try."

I catch his hands, holding onto him as if he's running out of the door. And on some level, I think he may be. "Why would you let Waters know things about you that I don't?" I gently but fiercely demand. "That gives him strength. That makes us weak. Just tell me everything and get it over with."

"Not tonight."

He means never, I think. "You'll have to tell me to testify."

His lips press together and he looks skyward, torment in his very existence and if I'm honest, it was there from the very moment I met him. Torment is a part of him. It lives inside him. It has become his own personal monster. "Adrian," I whisper softly.

He cups my face and looks at me. "I don't know if I have it in me to be without you anymore."

"Then don't," I say. "Don't."

His reply is to kiss me and murmur, "We need to rest. We'll talk tomorrow just as I promised."

I want to argue. I want to push him, but I'm aware of how late it is. I'm aware of the weariness in my mind and body, he must feel as well. I know those things lead us to no place good. And I fear tomorrow doesn't, either. I want tonight with him.

He pulls back the blanket on the opposite side of me and then he's maneuvered me underneath it and makes fast work of removing the robe again. He pulls me in front of him, my back to his front, and then leans over and shuts the light off. He still has on his jeans. As if he knows that's what I'm thinking, he says, "I won't let you sleep if I take them off."

"I'm not sure I care," I whisper.

"You will tomorrow." He strokes my hair. "Everything I do is to protect you, Pri. Don't forget that."

My lashes lower with the impact of those words.

Tomorrow, we will talk. Tomorrow, I won't like what he has to say. But I'm already feeling the calm, stronger me rise to the surface, and therefore, I know what Adrian does not. Tomorrow, I will kick his self-hatred to the curb. And when I do, we will kick Waters to the curb. We will win.

Chapter Nineteen

ADRIAN

My eyes open with the sound of my cell phone buzzing on the hotel nightstand. For just a moment, there is nothing but morning light and Pri still pressed close to me. Soft, sweet, strong, brave Priscilla Miller. The woman rocks my world. I lean in to nuzzle her neck but stop short.

Still, the phone buzzes, and while I resist the interruption, I know I can't ignore that call, not when we're hunted by assassins. As if proving that point, Pri's damn phone starts ringing as well, from the bathroom, I think. She moans and murmurs, "Make it stop."

"I wish I could, baby," I reply, kissing her neck and rolling away from her to grab my phone.

It stops ringing and starts all over again. I glance at the caller ID to find Blake's number. Pri snatches up the robe at the end of the bed and stands up, offering me a perfect view of her even more perfect heart-shaped ass. My cock is instantly standing at alert and yet I answer the damn call with a, "Morning, boss."

"I don't think you've ever called me boss," he says. "Interesting."

Pri disappears into the bathroom and I glance at the clock that reads eight AM. "Don't start psychoanalyzing me this early in the fucking morning." I sit up, scrubbing my jaw, still in the jeans I wore to bed. Last night, that decision made sense. In the morning light, when I have to have tough conversations with Pri, not so much.

"Sounds to me like Pri might have you thinking about staying around," Blake comments.

That apple falls close to the tree, but it's also soured before it ever hit the ground. "You know that's not an option for me."

"Nothing is possible if you decide it's impossible."

I grimace. "Are you auditioning to write fortune cookies or what?"

"Smartass," he grumbles. "Enough of that until later. I'm calling to officially give you a heads up. The lot of us will be there in your room in half an hour. You need to make a decision about Pri."

I don't have to ask what he means. We had this conversation last night. "You don't want to stay at the hotel?"

"It was a good move last night when we didn't have time to prep our team, but I asked our team assassin. Savage seems to think you're vulnerable in a hotel. And I got a second opinion and asked Seth, one of our former spooks. He said the same."

"And they suggest what?"

"Two options: a fancy flat on Fifth where we're well-sheltered, or your place, which has been carefully sheltered and prepped. You need to decide which."

The question of the hour—or rather, in this case, a half-hour. I know what I want to do. I know what I should do. Those two things conflict. I stand and watch the bathroom door for Pri's return as I ask, "Do you have an opinion on her safety?"

"Do you want me to tell you what to do?" Blake asks. "Because you know I am all about telling you what to do."

"This isn't about me, Blake."

"Isn't it?" he challenges.

My jaw tics. Pri exits the bathroom. Her hair has that wild, just fucked look. No, I amend, the wild, just fucked by me look that would have me ready to get her naked again, if she wasn't holding her phone, with her delicate brow furrowed. Something happened. Something always does.

"I have to go," I tell Blake. "I'll let you know when you get here." I disconnect. "What's wrong?" I ask, meeting Pri at the end of the bed.

"Logan left a voicemail." She punches play and the message begins.

"I told the police I shot myself. Because I'm protecting you, Pri. That's what I told you at the restaurant. All of this is to protect you. You have no idea just how much I've protected you. You need to come and see me and you need to do it now." The call disconnects.

"I don't have any idea how much he did to protect me?" she repeats. "What does that mean, Adrian? Are my parents more involved in this than I know about? Because damn it, I already barely know how to save them."

I catch her arms and step into her. "I don't know, but we'll find out and if we can save them, we'll save them."

"Only we won't. I know that deep in my gut, the way I suspect you knew it with your brother."

"I did," I say, "but I fought for him until the last minute, until that was no longer possible, and that's what we'll do for your family."

"*We?*" she challenges.

I don't even hesitate as I confirm, "We. And that includes me and all of the Walker team, who will be here in about twenty minutes."

Her eyes go wide. "Twenty minutes? The entire team? What's going on?"

"We're going to game plan together and then move locations."

"Move where?"

"To be determined," I say, backing her up into the bathroom. "We should shower together to save time." I untie the robe and settle my hands on her shoulders, easing the terry cloth down and letting it fall to the ground, my gaze raking hungrily over her puckered nipples.

"Adrian," she whispers, and I fold her close, my blood hot, my body hard, my heart completely at her mercy.

My fingers tangle in her soft, dark locks. "I will never get tired of you saying my name." And then I kiss her, drinking her in, some might say avoiding the topic of what comes next. But I'm not. What comes next is us under a hot spray of water, her pressed in the corner, and me pressed inside her.

That is what comes next.

Chapter Twenty

ADRIAN

I fuck Pri in that shower as if I will never fuck her, let alone make love to her, again. And maybe I won't. I drive into her, her leg at my hip, water flowing over us, with the fierceness of a man who must have it all, all of her. When it's over, we don't speak but it's in the air—it being all the things we haven't talked about but will soon.

Don't ask me how we manage to get dressed by the time Blake and the crew arrive, but we do. With my direction, and a need to stay neutral to draw as little attention as possible, both of us dress in black jeans and black T-shirts.

"I'm sure Savage will tell us how cute we are," Pri comments, pulling on a pair of lace-up ankle boots.

"I'm sure he will," I agree, "but Savage can kiss my ass."

She laughs. "Careful with that offer. He might just do it."

"Thems fighting words," I joke, as a knock sounds on the door. "And that will be the team," I say.

Pri motions to her wet hair. "I won't blend in like this on a winter day."

"Finish up," I say, kissing her. "Just come on out when you're ready."

With that, I leave Pri in the bathroom and shut the bedroom door. For a moment, I just stand there, in no rush to answer the door. My place or the safe house? I decide on the safe house for one reason: Pri is going to hate me for what I'm about to suggest. I don't want her to feel trapped in my territory.

Decision made, the knocking has started again, and I head for the door, checking the peephole before opening up. Blake is the first inside the room, with Savage and Adam following. Savage is holding a coat in his hands. "Candace sent this for Pri." He sets it on a chair.

Blake indicates bags in his hands. "Donuts."

Adam sets two trays of Starbucks coffee on the table. "Caffeine," he says, indicating one tray to add, "White mocha," then the other, "Cinnamon dolce."

Since I didn't exactly sleep last night, at least not well, I grab a white mocha and sip. "What's new, if anything?" I ask, sitting on the arm of a chair while Savage grabs a coffee and sits down across from me.

"Not much," Adam says, grabbing a cinnamon dolce himself, and plopping down on the couch.

Savage opens the box of donuts and grabs an éclair. "Fuck yeah," he says, and I don't disagree, and neither does my stomach. I grab a glazed donut and take a bite.

"An accurate statement," Blake says, ignoring the coffee to sit down next to Adam. "Both about the donuts," he grabs a glazed himself, "and an update. All is quiet right now. Almost too fucking quiet, if you ask me."

I've pretty much inhaled the donut and finish it off. "Logan called Pri. Something about protecting her more than she knows. I don't know what that prick's story is, but he's trouble. And I don't think her parents are being blackmailed. I think they're willing participants."

"Lucifer's been up all night trying to identify the bald man," Blake says, already on donut number two. "He's got it in his head that if we find him, we find Deleon."

"If we find him, I'm killing him," I say, my gaze meeting Blake's, "and feel free to fire me after, *boss*."

Blake sips his coffee and Savage says, "Fuck yeah, you were right, boss. He's staying."

"Agreed," Adam concurs. "He wants to stay. I just wonder if I can get him to call me boss?"

Savage grabs another donut. "Just call me daddy." He wiggles his eyebrows and eyes the group. "This is an appetizer, right? We're ordering breakfast when we get where we're going?"

"You had breakfast," Adam reminds him and then adds, "And that daddy joke is weird, but then, what do I expect? You're weird, Savage."

I ignore them all. "Assume her parents are dirty," I say.

"That statement sounds like—pretend she's pretty," Savage comments dryly. "When she's not pretty."

Sometimes I have no fucking clue what Savage is talking about. "I agree with Adam. You're weird, Savage. I need to save her parents. If it's possible, I need *us* to save them."

"You can't," Savage says. "We can't. You can't save people who don't want to be saved."

"Now you have to make sense?" I challenge.

"I always make sense," he says, dusting icing from his hands. "Save her. That's who you need to save."

"We'll save them if we can," Blake interjects, "but right now, Savage is right. We need to save Pri." He looks between us all. "The question is how? She's now a target. Waters has power from the inside. How do we do that?"

"The way I see it," Adam says, setting his cup down, "Waters dies, which obviously isn't an option or Pri leaves town and changes her name when this is all over. Preferably with her own personal bodyguard—you."

Now, I set my cup down, hands on my thighs. "I don't want her to have to give up her life."

"Then you need to write us a story here with a happy ending," Savage challenges. "And write it snap, crackle, and pop, as in right now."

"All right," I say. "She has to drop the case and then blame me for turning on her. She has to turn me into the enemy and do so publicly."

"*Drop the case*? Are you kidding me?"

At the sound of Pri's indignant voice, I turn to find her standing in the doorway, the pink of anger shading her cheeks. "I'm not dropping the case," she assures me, "and if that means I have to leave the country, I'll leave. I'm not sure there was ever another option, and on some level, I knew that. But I leave when Waters is in jail for the rest of his life and not a minute sooner."

I stand and Pri is now beside me, just at the edge of the coffee table. Her chin lifts defiantly and her eyes meet mine. "I'm not dropping the case."

"You have to consider—"

"No," she says. "You know that means he goes free."

That's the idea, I think, but I'm not going to admit that to her or anyone else. "We'll talk."

"We just did." She eyes the coffee and says, "Please tell me one of those is for me."

"White mocha or cinnamon dolce?" Adam asks, indicating the appropriate trays.

Pri grabs a white mocha. "Thank you," she says, sipping the hot beverage and ignoring me. "I understand the hotel is no longer safe?"

"Speaking as an assassin, or rather an ex-assassin," Savage amends, "I don't do that shit anymore, I'm a new man now, but when I *was* that guy, I loved hotel hits. The staff rotates, chatters for the right price, and makes it easy to blend in and sneak right on inside your target's private space."

"Somehow I don't think you're a guy who blends in," Pri comments.

"Better than you might think," Savage replies, eyeing me.

"What he's saying," Blake interjects, "is that hotels can work, but not with this level of a contract hit in play. One night is fine. Two is not."

She sips her coffee. "Then where to now?"

Blake's eyes meet mine and my prior plan goes out the door. I give him a lift of the chin and he needs no more. And I swear that bastard's lips quirk with amusement. Fuck him. I don't care what he thinks right now. I care about Pri. And I'm going to make her listen to reason if I have to tie her to my damn bed. It's where I've wanted her anyway.

LISA RENEE JONES

108

Chapter Twenty-One

ADRIAN

At this point, we're huddled in the center of the hotel living room drinking coffee while an assassin could be plotting a way to get to us. "We have to assume we've been followed. What's the plan to get us all the hell out of here?"

Blake sips his coffee and gives a bag by the chair a nudge with his foot. "Adam brought his bag of disguises. He's going to dress you two up all pretty."

"Easier to do with Pri," Adam says, giving me side-eye. "*You* are another story. We'll forget pretty and just stick to making you a different shade of ugly."

"You only wish you were my kind of pretty," I say, patting my cheek. "That's why you're always playing dress-up."

He laughs and motions for Pri to sit in a chair and for once, she obeys, probably because it's not me dishing out the orders.

Savage steps closer and gives me and then Pri a quick inspection before he grins. "Just so you know, it didn't go unnoticed. You two look so darn cute in your matching black outfits," Savage chimes in. "Twins like Adam and Eve, only they were naked."

"Jesus, Savage," Adam murmurs, kneeling in front of Pri.

"I'm not sure He was there," Savage replies. "Not in the Garden."

"Adam and Eve were not twins," Pri points out. "That's weird, Savage."

"Ignore Savage," Adam instructs Pri, unzipping his bag. "That's what the rest of us do."

Blake walks out on the patio and does whatever it is Blake does. I stand behind Pri, watching Adam work, listening to him interact with Pri. We've all asked her to trust us to keep her alive. I've asked her to trust *me* to such a degree that I want her to walk away from Waters. And I am not sure I've given her enough of me to deserve that trust. The problem is that once I do, I may end up losing what she's given me. And her.

I almost laugh at the idea that I tried to walk away from her last night. Like that is ever fucking happening.

It's not.

Ever.

Happening.

A few minutes later, Pri is in a red wig with a shoulder-length bob style, a pink coat, and pink lipstick.

"You're done," Adam says, standing to allow her to do the same. "Go take a look in the mirror and get comfortable with the new you."

She stands up and turns toward the bedroom, only to run right into me. I catch her arms, and her lips part in surprise, the heat of anger and attraction ripe between us. And damn it, she's just as pretty as a redhead. She's just so fucking perfect, too damn perfect for the likes of me and she doesn't seem to care.

"I didn't know you were there," she murmurs softly.

"And yet, I am," I say, and it's a complicated statement that reaches well beyond this moment in time. She knows it, too. I see it in the slight flicker of awareness in her eyes. But this is not a new revelation between us. We have always been complicated. We have always been forbidden. And when you cross those kinds of lines, the forbidden kind, there are consequences. And we are now living those consequences in the way of Waters' attention on Pri, which I must find a way to shift.

I release her and for a moment she just stares at me, a mix of turbulent emotions in her eyes, before her chin dips and she steps around me. I want to pull her back. I want to follow her. I don't know if I've ever wanted so many fucking things as I do with Pri all the damn time.

The bedroom door shuts behind me, and the room's attention is fixed on me. Savage grins and grabs what has to be his sixth donut. "It's getting hot in here," he sings, quoting what I think is supposed to be an old Nelly song. "I want to take off all my clothes."

"Please don't," Adam says, as the bedroom door is already opening again.

I shift my footing to bring Pri into view as she motions up and down her body. "I feel like I stand out in this outfit," she worries. "Red and pink?"

"Would you ever dress like that?" Adam asks.

Her brows dip. "Well, no, but—"

"Then you've already answered your question," Adam replies. "You don't look like you. That means you look perfect."

She inhales sharply and concedes. "If you're really certain."

"I am," Adam assures her.

"If only you were that agreeable with me," I comment.

"I have a reply in my head," Pri says, "that I'll save for that warm and fuzzy moment when we're alone."

"I'm sure I can't wait," I reply dryly, and the truth is, I can't fucking wait.

"You look good, chica," Savage chimes in. "I'd let you live. Eat a donut," he adds. "Live your life. We're going to make sure you keep it."

"Stop talking, Savage," I say.

Adam motions for me to sit. "The sooner we get this done, the sooner we can stop listening to him talk."

"Agreed," I say, claiming the chair.

A few quick minutes later, Pri is drinking her coffee, watching me transform into Adam's vision of a new me. Soon, I'm sporting salt and pepper in my goatee, while I'm wearing a top hat, a thick double-breasted jacket, and some kind of pointed-toe black shoes.

Savage, of course, offers his commentary. "You look like one of those creepy professors at the universities that fucks all his students and then claims he didn't."

"Thank you, Savage," I say tightly.

He raises his cup in my direction. "Just keeping it real, man," he says, while Pri laughs, but the sound is strained, almost choked.

She's nervous and dressing up like strangers isn't helping. Her laughter fades and her eyes meet mine, and the tension between us is just too damn taut. She's pissed and stubborn and there is a fight in our future that cannot be avoided. I'm going to save her life even if she hates me for it.

Chapter Twenty-Two

ADRIAN

I'm about ten seconds from pulling Pri into the bedroom and kissing the hell out of her, or just plain kissing her right here in front of everyone when Blake returns from outside. "Let's get the fuck out of Dodge," he calls out, and just like that, the moment between me and Pri is lost.

Suddenly the team huddles around us, and as it should be, Blake's focus is on Pri. "I want you to walk through the lobby," he instructs her, "and ask the doorman where the nearest Starbucks is. Walk to that Starbucks and go inside. It's a block down and a block to the right. It's close."

My objection is instant. "No," I say. "I don't want her out in the open on her own. I'll go with her."

"Nada, man," Savage interjects. "You two together is an assassin's wet dream. Two paydays in one place. Split up. You need to split up."

"It's the right move," Blake argues. "And our team is spread out along the path we have her traveling."

"Damn it," I murmur, scrubbing the back of my neck because they're right, but the memory of Logan following Pri into that bathroom is crystal clear and pretty damn awful. "Her purse is gone. She needs a new one and a gun to put inside it."

"Ask and you shall receive," Adam says, producing a pink handbag. "A loaner from Luke's wife, Julie." He hands the purse to Pri. "There's a baby Glock inside. I realize, based on the weapon you carry, that isn't your favored handgun, but that's the best we could do on short notice."

Pri blinks and accepts the bag. "She loaned me a pink Louis Vuitton you can no longer purchase? Now I really need a bodyguard. Or to bribe her to keep it."

"Check the weapon," I say because I know Pri well enough to know that she's talking about the purse to distract herself from what comes next, and I can't let her entertain that kind of headspace. Not now. Not when I need her to be ready for anything. "Make sure you're comfortable handling it."

She settles the purse on her shoulder and removes the Glock, checking the ammo with a skill that I'm certain no one in this room misses. "It's good," she declares. "It's a little large for my hand, but I've practiced with one a few times. I can manage."

I give a nod and glance at Blake. "Where am I when she's in the lobby and walking to Starbucks?"

"You'll exit the hotel through the side door, and you can walk the parallel street to the Starbucks," he says, "but don't join her inside the coffee shop. Watch her from across the street. Once she's safely in the car with me, walk a block east, and we'll have a car waiting on you. You and Pri will reconnect at the safe house."

"What happens to Pri once she gets to Starbucks?" I ask.

"She orders," Adam interjects. "I'll already be inside the coffee shop, and I won't be in disguise." He glances at Pri and adds, "I don't want you to have to hunt for me. But don't talk to me or approach me."

She nods and folds her arms in front of her, and focuses on Blake. "How do I pay for the order? I'll have no money."

Blake reaches into a bag on the coffee table and hands her a cellphone. "This is yours to keep."

"I have one Adam gave me."

"Out of an abundance of caution, we're changing it out again," he replies. "And yes, all your calls are masked and forwarded, just as before. You'll find a Starbucks app set up as Paige West. Pay that way. As long as you're here in the city, you're Paige. There's a wallet in your purse with an ID that validates your identity. You'll need to keep that wig and use it."

He then grabs another phone from the bag and hands it to me. "Your replacement for the phone you threw away back in Austin. Everything is plugged in already."

"And after I order?" Pri queries, obviously no longer about distraction but rather the plan. "What next?"

"You pick up your drink," Blake says, "exit the store, and walk to the black sedan that will be waiting on you by the curb with me inside." His eyes meet mine. "We'll be on her like a bee on honey, man. She'll be safe."

And yet, Logan still got to her last night, I think, but I keep that to myself. Pri doesn't need another reason to be nervous. I glance around the room and focus on Blake. "I need a minute with Pri."

Chapter Twenty-Three

ADRIAN

Blake motions for the team to head for the door. In a quick rush of activity, they grab our bags and their supplies. Blake drops two sealed bags with earpieces in them on the table. "Take ten, then move. We'll be in position."

"Got it," I say, but Blake doesn't leave.

He steps toe-to-toe with me. "You're not used to having a team you can trust. You do now. "

He's wrong. I've had people I trusted. The problem is that trust has become a reoccurring theme in my life of friendship, betrayal, love, and loss. I didn't think I'd trust again, ever, but then Blake and these hard heads at Walker don't like to take no for an answer.

His eyes narrow on mine as if he's read my thoughts. His lips quirk slightly before he glances at Pri and says, "The next half hour will suck, but it's just a half-hour. Once you're in the safe house, no one is going to find you."

"I know," Pri says, standing a little straighter as she does. "I just want to do this and get it over with and then laugh at myself in the red wig."

Blake gives her a little nod and then looks at me, a promise in his stare to protect her before he backs away and disappears inside the foyer.

Pri and I turn to each other, the air instantly charged, anger flickering in her eyes, no less hot than the heat of desire there, too, desire she can try to deny, but she'll fail. The minute the door opens and shuts, she says, "You need to know—"

"I know," I say, and I scoop Pri into my arms, one hand between her shoulder blades, the other cupping her neck. "I *know* you hate me right now, but—"

"*Hate you?*" she asks incredulously. "I don't hate you. I'm angry with you, but that isn't hate. You should have talked to me, not them, about my decisions, and about what's best for me and us. And we're going to fight about it later, in the safe house."

"In my apartment."

She pulls back and studies me, blinking in confusion. "Your apartment?"

"Yes. *My apartment.* Where I will keep you forever if that's what it takes to keep you safe."

"And if I won't stay?"

"I'll convince you," I assure her.

"And if you can't?" she challenges.

I have a vision of her tied to my bed, which I don't think she'd appreciate right about now, so I repeat, "*I'll convince you,* Pri."

Her eyes narrow, awareness in their depths. "Never cage an angry woman. You need to learn that and so does Waters. She won't play nice. *I* won't play nice, Adrian."

My hand finds the back of that red wig and I lean in close. "Is that a promise?"

"Yes," she says. "It's absolutely a promise."

I lean in to kiss her and she presses her fingers to my mouth. "Red lipstick and not the stay-on kind."

"That's your only objection?"

"We might die. That makes me liberal with my kisses, but that doesn't mean you can kiss me when this is over."

"We aren't going to die, and with you, baby, I will take what I can get." I pull her hand back and kiss the hell out of her, drinking her in, consuming her, possessing her, and when she moans, I part our lips and say, "That shit about not knowing what this is was bullshit to protect you. You know that, right?"

"I know enough," she whispers. "Call Blake. Let me just do this. I have a fight with you at your place to get to."

I hesitate on her "I know enough" reply, but this isn't the time or place for this conversation. I kiss her again, hard and fast before I grab the earpieces and help her place hers properly.

"Talk to us. Tell us what you see. Tell us what your instincts tell you. We'll be close. I'll be close. Understand?"

She nods. That's all, just a nod. No words.

She's focused on what is before us, probably fighting nerves. I install my headset and signal our readiness to the team before I wipe wayward lipstick from above her lip. "You look like you've been kissing some asshole."

"I have," she assures me, with a hint of a nervous smile. "Is it all over my face?"

"No. I got you," I promise, and I'm not just talking about the lipstick.

Her eyes warm and she motions to my mouth. "You have a few hints of pink on your lips."

"I don't mind looking like I've been kissing a pretty woman." I motion her toward the exit.

She nods and we enter the foyer, pausing at the door, where she draws in a sharp breath and turns to me, poking my chest. "Do not get killed or arrested, Adrian Mack. Do you understand?"

I capture her hand. "Yes, ma'am."

She glares at me for obvious impact and then turns and opens the door. The minute it closes behind her, I swear I'm losing my mind. I scrub a hand through my hair and promise myself that she's safe. She is so fucking safe. We'll be in my apartment fighting and fucking in no time.

It can be no other way.

Or I might go on a damn killing streak that will put Savage to shame.

Chapter Twenty-Four

PRI

I step into the empty elevator car and remind myself that I have to own the moment when I exit to the lobby as surely as I own the courtroom when I deliver an opening or closing statement. As a prosecutor, even if I'm not sold on my position, I have to sell it. And right now, I have to sell Paige, the redhead with pink lipstick. The elevator is modern and speedy and it's time to execute my ownership of Paige a little too quickly. Nonetheless, the doors open and my heart flutters at the idea of a killer in wait for me. Shoving that horrid thought aside, I exit the elevator and lift my chin a little higher, a façade of confidence my friend, as I tell myself to enjoy wearing pink instead of boring, professional black, and navy.

Remembering Adrian's warning about a traveling gaze drawing attention, I travel the lobby without a glance at anyone else, certain Paige would have nothing but her need for Starbucks on her mind anyway. Oh to be that carefree in real life right now, able to enjoy the sweet thrill of coffee without fear of death. I've actually never been what anyone would call carefree. I like having a case to fret over. I need a purpose at all times. And prosecuting Waters is my purpose now. I will never walk away. The fact that I'm in a wig, forced to run for my life, doesn't change that. It just reminds me of his pure evil and enforces why I can't back down.

I can't believe Adrian would believe I'd do otherwise.

Anger burns in my belly, and with it, courage swells—I'm fighting this monster and I will not cower. Adrian won't convince me to do otherwise.

With the newfound push of rebellion charging my footsteps, I move a little quicker as I spy the doorman, a short man with a shiny bald head, and step right into his path. "Excuse me, sir."

His rather beady brown eyes fix on me and I look for some strange reaction to a woman in a wig, but if he notices, he offers no indication. "Yes, miss," he says. "What can I do for you?"

I blink with the use of the word "miss," which is unfamiliar as it applies to me. Obviously, the hair and outfit affect perception—a comforting thought that confirms I don't look like myself.

"You can save me from crashing and burning," I say. "I'm desperate for caffeine. Can you direct me to the nearest Starbucks?"

"Of course," he says, smiling a friendly smile. "Gotta have that caffeine fix." He points me in the expected direction. "That way to heaven."

Hopefully, not in a literal way, I think, shoving aside that daunting thought.

Thanking the doorman, I step away from him, and there is a slight prickling of my skin and I suppress the need to respond with a cursory glance around the lobby, telling myself that of course I'm being watched—the Walker team is, in fact, watching me. Hurrying toward the exit, I enter the revolving doors, preparing myself for the cold New York City day, busy streets, and potential assassins waiting for me outside. The instant my foot hits the sidewalk, the cold is colder than expected, sideswiping me with biting air. I snuggle deeper into my coat, turn right, and start walking.

Blake's voice sounds in my ear. "I've got eyes on you all the way to Starbucks and even when you go inside."

This news is comforting, as is the cold weather that offers me an excuse to walk faster than would be normal. And so, I do. I hurry forward, melting into the folds of the thick crowd, seeking the shelter of many, and hoping my prospective killer will not as well. Fortunately, I live through the short walk and break from the crowd to approach the Starbucks door. That's when a man blasts out of nowhere and knocks into me. I gasp at the impact and then his hands are on my shoulders.

Adrenaline surges through me, my instincts screaming that this is trouble. "Easy there, miss," purrs a cigarette-roughened voice, and then I'm staring into icy blues eyes framed by a well-lined face. There is something brutal and hard in those eyes.

I jerk back from his touch. "Sorry about that."

"Just be careful," he says, and his lips quirk as he adds, "I wouldn't want you to get hurt."

In that moment, Savage steps to my side, his big body nudging mine to the right, toward the Starbucks. "Hello, Michael," he says, and his voice is as cold as the ice in the other man's eyes. I gasp with the realization that he knows this stranger, and that this stranger must have come here for me.

Michael is an assassin.

My heart thunders in my chest and I turn for the Starbucks entrance, seeking shelter, but I never make it inside. The door opens and Adam steps out. The next thing I know, he's placed me between him and the wall, ushering me forward. In a blink, we turn the corner, and then I'm pulled into the alcove of some sort of business or residential space. Adam disappears and Adrian grabs me, pulling me to him.

"What just happened?" I ask, urgently, when it's really a nonsense question. We both know what happened.

Still, I do revel in his confidently spoken reply. "Nothing we weren't ready for and now we maneuver accordingly." He removes my wig, tossing it behind him, somewhere inside the alcove, and then he's reaching for my coat. "It's going to be a cold walk out of here, but you have to get rid of this." He tugs at the buttons and slides the coat down my shoulders.

A part of me resists losing that coat, and not because I'm a Texas girl who hates the cold, but rather, because it feels like a shield that protects me beyond the weather. Still, I do as is necessary. I shrug out of it and Adrian dumps it behind him before he shrugs out of his own jacket, pulling it around me. "This will be better than nothing," he says, urging me to push my hands through the oversized sleeves.

"We're going into the subway," he explains, rolling up the sleeves above my hands. "Just stay close and don't look around. Looking around gains attention. Trust me and the team to know what is happening. And Adam won't be far behind us. Got it?"

I nod. "Yes. I'm good. Let's just do it."

There's a hint of something in his brown eyes that I can't quite read—respect, I think—and appreciate, though I'm wondering if I really deserve it. I did secretly want a coat of armor.

Adrian leans out of the alcove, scans the area a moment, and then he's leading me onto the sidewalk and into a brisk, cold wind, and he does so in only his shirt sleeves. If he notices the wintry day, he never hunches, never indicates discomfort, but then right now, I'm not cold either. Adrenaline burns hot through my blood, along with a hefty dose of nerves and a bit of fear. I hate the fear, but it's hard not to think about the fact that I just had an assassin's hands on my body. And that at any moment, a bullet could hit one of us, or both of us, if the assassin knows just when and where to place the shot.

Chapter Twenty-Five

PRI

A few short blocks later, Adrian leads me into the subway tunnel and we disappear beneath the protection of the concrete structure. Once there, though, there's little time to revel in any relief that shelter offers as we rush down the stairs and Adrian bypasses the need to buy passes. We reach the security gate and he lifts me over the top and then side hurdles it himself. Grabbing my hand again, we run for the stairs. The train is already loaded, the buzzer warning of the doors closing, but Adrian guides me inside anyway, catching the doors as they try to shut on us.

The car is empty and Adrian grabs a pole and pulls me in front of it on the opposite side, cupping my head and bringing our foreheads together. "I should never have let you make that walk alone."

Because he needs to protect me from all the demons and monsters, including himself. I shove away that emotionally packed premise and pull back to ask him the obvious question. "What went wrong?"

"It's not what went wrong. It's what went right. We're still alive. And that says a lot when you're defending a hit placed on the dark web, you're dealing with expert hackers, trackers, and killers."

"And yet we hid in plain sight. We shouldn't have gone to the hotel."

"Wrong. We needed to fish out a problem and we damn sure didn't want to lead anyone to my apartment."

There's logic there, I think, perhaps flawed logic, but for now, I focus on the future. "How do we know they won't find us now or once we get there?"

"No one will find my apartment. We just need to make sure we're not followed." The car halts and he kisses me, and then once again captures my hand. "Hold on tight. It's going to be a long few hours."

And then we're moving again, exiting the car, hurrying toward the train just across from us, going back in the direction we just came from.

Two hours later, we've not only changed trains six times, we've walked at least a few miles in between train stations before reentering the subway to start all over again. When I'm sure we're about to call this done and go to his place, he leads me into a pizza joint inside the subway tunnels. "Let's grab some food and do some people watching."

"Are you sure we should be eating right now?"

"Now is the perfect time," he assures me, pulling me in front of him at the counter, the press of his big body behind me almost sweet enough for me to forget we're being hunted. My nostrils flare with the scent of pizza cooking and I order a slice of cheese. Adrian orders two pepperoni. With our food in hand, Adrian directs me to a small table with a view of the restaurant, and the people walking past the window in the tunnels. We sit side by side and my stomach groans with the need for food.

I pick up my slice and take a bite. Adrian does the same, his gaze on the space before us. His phone buzzes with a text. I watch him remove his phone from his pocket and type one word: *Clear.*

"Blake," he informs me without me asking. "The headset isn't working in the tunnel. That's why we've been on silent."

His phone buzzes with another message. He reads it and then shows it to me. That's Adam. The message reads simply: *Clear.*

"Is he still shadowing us?" I ask.

"He's somewhere close," he confirms, and while I'm comforted by this idea, I'm aware that he doesn't appear near at all. Which means someone else could pull off that same magical feat.

Perhaps Michael could pull off that magical feat, and so I dare ask, "And Savage? Do we have any idea where he is right now?"

He arches a brow at me. "You mean, where is Michael?"

"I looked into that man's eyes. He's a killer."

"So is Savage. And Savage is dealing with him. And no, you and I don't want to know any details. Michael won't be a problem again. That's enough." His eyes meet mine. "Some things are just better left alone."

In other words, he has no intention of ever trusting me enough to tell me about his brother. He will never really be mine. He will always find a way to hate himself enough to leave me. Because leaving me is saving me.

Adrian and I don't speak for the rest of the meal.

The restaurant is empty and yet he watches the empty seats and the tunnel. I watch the restaurant and the tunnel. When it's time to leave, I point to the bathroom. "Can I go?"

"I'll go with you."

He grabs our trash and dumps it, and then follows me to the bathrooms. Once we're there, he says, "Me first. I want to be sure I have eyes on the room when you're inside." He opens the unisex door. "Stand in the doorway with it cracked. Watch for trouble."

I nod and give him my back. He's done quickly and catches me from behind, his hands on my body, even in these dire times, a snap of heat I feel in the most intimate of ways.

"Your turn," he says, and when he releases me, I disappear into the bathroom. He shuts the door, offers me privacy and I hurry through the necessities. When I'm done, I exit the bathroom and he surprises me by pulling me in front of him, tunneling his fingers into my hair, and bringing my lips to his lips. "You have changed me in ways you may never understand." And then his mouth closes down on mine, and his tongue licks into my mouth in a kiss that is not just a kiss. This is his story, it's our story, and that story is about hopes and desires, torment and passion. It's a kiss that devours me, takes from me, and when it's over, leaves me wanting more. Leaves me with more questions than answers.

For a moment, we just breathe together, and Adrian gently brushes my hair from my face, tucking it behind my ear, his gaze lifting and scanning the restaurant before he says, "We have to go."

"I know," I say, wishing it were not true, wishing I could just hold him here, right here, no matter where we are, and ask those questions. But they are not for now. Maybe they will not be for the future. Because maybe that's all Adrian will ever be for me: a question that was never answered.

Chapter Twenty-Six

PRI

Another hour and a half later, Adrian and I are on the street again, in an area where high-rise buildings prevail and saltwater permeates in the air from the nearby water.

We turn down a side street, walking up a hill, and Adrian leads me into a small alleyway beside a shorter brick building—well, at least compared to the high-rises, and it seems to sit almost on stilts, with open space beneath it. To my surprise, we head down a set of stairs and pause at a door, where he keys in a code.

"What is this place?" I ask.

"Home sweet home, baby," he replies with a wink. "And if you didn't notice, we have a museum and bank on either side of us, which makes it easy to piggyback onto their security and cameras." He holds open the door and I enter to find an elevator waiting on us.

Adrian is quickly behind me, and I watch him secure the door again with another code. And then there's yet one more code for the elevator. The doors open quickly and Adrian motions me forward. I quickly enter the car and he joins me. "There's a pizza in our future. Tell me you want pizza."

"Didn't we just eat pizza a few hours ago?" I ask.

131

"That was *not* pizza," he says as the doors close. "More like cardboard."

The elevator starts to move and there is only one floor, and that's the top floor.

Adrian's phone buzzes with a text. He removes it from his pocket. "I'll order you some real pizza," he says, glancing down at the message.

I want to be nonchalant like him. I want to think about pizza and him and us but instead, I have two things on my mind: that message and the assassins hunting us.

"Everything okay?" I ask apprehensively.

"Just our team confirming they're securing the building behind us." The elevator halts. "Let me clear the building before you exit." He steps toward me and settles a comfortable, possessive hand on my hip. "We're safe. I designed this place from scratch with a little help from the Walker team. And as for now, tonight, Walker had security set-up before we ever got here and this check I'm about to do is just me being extra careful because you're here. Okay?"

"Yes," I assure him quickly, aware of the tenderness in him in this moment, a gentleness that contrasts that darker side of Adrian. The caveat is that I see both parts of him while he only sees the dark side. And both parts of him so easily seduce me beyond the reason I value. And usually, I don't even care, not with him, but here, in his home, and with so much on the line, I do tonight.

At this point, the elevator doors are open and he punches a hold button. "I'll be fast," he says, disappearing into his apartment. *His* apartment. This is an invitation to see his world, to know him on a different level, but I'm suddenly wondering if that was the problem on the plane tonight. Did the idea of me coming here give him cold feet and regrets about us?

Did he push that uncertainty between us about love and our future to remove any chance I'd feel like his home sweet home was mine?

Suddenly, I'm repeating his own words in my mind. *Some things are better left alone.*

There are so many meanings I could assign to that statement right here and now if I let my mind go wild, and it's good at doing that. I make a living letting my mind go wild to uncover harsh facts.

Time ticks by, too much time, and my heart begins to thunder in my chest. What if a surprise awaited him inside? What if Adrian's in trouble? What if he needs my help? I unzip my purse and remove my weapon. Adrian appears in the elevator doors and glances at the gun, a pulse of that dark energy in the air, as his brown eyes meet mine. "What's that for?"

"I thought you might need to be saved."

His eyes narrow and there's a tick of something more in the air now. "And you were going to save me?"

"Yes," I say simply, returning the Glock to my purse and zipping it up. "Thankfully, I didn't need to shoot someone else in the foot."

I expect him to laugh or smile, but he doesn't. He just looks at me, studies me a beat and then a beat longer, his expression unreadable, but somehow punched with an eruption of emotion. "Come inside. I'll pour us some whiskey. We both need a drink right about now."

He backs away, disappears, an invitation in that action.

I don't immediately move.

Instead, Adrian's own words are back in my head: *You have changed me in ways you will never understand.* Somehow, I know that once I enter his apartment, I will not leave the same person.

Chapter Twenty-Seven

PRI

The truth is that I was a changed person the moment I met Adrian.

I was a blank canvas that had been colored in the grays and blacks of betrayal and distrust. He'd splashed that canvas with colors, the sunshine to the stormy nights that had become my days, even if I had not seen that reality.

And as my father said to me when I was first learning to practice law: *You can't look back. You can't turn back. Go forward and use what you've learned, even the mistakes.* I don't know where Adrian and I are going, but I'm not looking back.

Therefore, with nerves in my belly, I enter his world. I step off the elevator and into his apartment, a dark stained concrete floor beneath my feet. Adrian is immediately behind me, reaching for the oversized jacket I'm wearing and easing it down my shoulders. I steel myself for the touch of his skin to mine, but disappointedly, it doesn't follow.

"I turned on the fireplace remotely before we got here," he says, and I believe he's hanging the jacket on a coat rack. "The apartment should be warm."

I don't rotate to face him. Instead, I hug myself, a protective gesture born of the vulnerability I've felt with Adrian since our incident on the plane. I don't know who or what we are anymore, and I could tell myself to live in the moment, but it's not that simple. Not for me and Adrian.

His hand settles on my hip, hand flattening on my back, a hot possessiveness in the unexpected touch that should perhaps not be unexpected at all. I'm in his apartment. One might say that he's touched me over and over these past few hours, but this touch is different: it commands, it demands, it assumes ownership. No. No, that's not right. Logan's touch assumed ownership, and I hated it. Adrian's touch is a possession created by us, not him, a product of our intense connection. And we *do have* an intense connection, of this, I do not question.

He shifts and stands in front of me, studies me, and I can almost taste the words on his lips, and the hesitation that flavors them. "I'll get that whiskey."

I decide whiskey is just fine by me. I need to relax. I need to come down from whatever this emotional ride I'm taking with this man is. I nod my approval and then his hand is gone, leaving behind a hot burn and my puckered nipples. Lord help me, I'm so damn out of my head and inside my body right now, which isn't a safe place to be. Not when our lives are on the line and big decisions have to be made and made with urgency.

I watch him cross the room, long, confident strides, a lethal glide to his steps. Only then do I take in the room, notice the masculine space of dark colors accented by a stained concrete floor of browns and tans. The living room is before me, brown couches framing floor-to-ceiling windows with a view of the water, while two winding staircases sit left and right in the rear of the space. To my right is the kitchen with a dark, round wooden island covered in stone.

Adrian heads toward that living room and to the bar on the far side of it just beneath one of those winding stairwells. I draw a deep breath and follow him, noting the thick tan and cream rug beneath the couches, the fireplace that lines the entire center wall beneath the windows that don't quite reach the concrete floor. The room is cozy, sitting on top of the ocean, or so the stunning view suggests. We're higher than I thought. This place is expensive and I'm reminded of his overseas jobs for big money. I know his plan without even asking. I've heard enough to assume.

Kill Waters.

Leave the country.

Damn him, no.

I'm confused and angry and confused all over again. We have to talk about this, really talk. I hurry forward and sit on one of two stools at the concrete-finished bar, the counter smooth beneath my palms, where I steady my hands. Adrian immediately sets a glass in front of me. "That's a peach whiskey. It's smooth and goes down easily."

He's watching me, his eyes warm on my face. I reach for the glass and sip, the sweet flavor on my tongue welcome, the bite that follows not as intense as I expect. "It's good," I say, and I quickly sip again, bigger, deeper before I blurt, "I'm not going to drop the case."

He arches his brow. "That's been on your mind all these hours, hasn't it?"

"Are you surprised?"

"No. It's been on my mind, too."

"I don't know how you believe I could or would," I say. "We both know Waters cannot walk free."

"He might as well be free now. He's behind bars, festering with anger, and using that anger to find ways to hunt down and kill his enemies. He's not weak inside that prison. He might even be stronger. So, yes, I know he'd go free."

"Free is free. At least he has some limitations now."

"The only limitation that matters with him is life or death, baby. You have to know that."

My eyes narrow. "What does that mean?" I ask, but I know. I know oh so well where he's going with this.

"He has enemies out here. He has servants inside, servants who fear him. Let him go free, where his enemies who do not fear him can get to him."

"You mean *you*?" I challenge.

"Whoever gets to him first."

"You can't *kill him*."

He says nothing. He just stares at me.

"Adrian," I press softly.

"He's killed your witnesses. He'll kill whoever he needs to kill to survive. He'll kill you if I let him. And I won't. I will do whatever is necessary to give you your life back. So, drop the case, Pri. Drop it and let me handle this."

"That is not the right answer. *No.* That is not what you or I stand for."

"He can get to us right now, but we can't get to him. Some decisions are about survival."

"Is this why we're here instead of someplace else? For you to convince me to do things your way?"

His expression hardens, his voice with it. "That's what you think, Pri?" His jaw flexes. His eyes burn with something that reads like anger. "Of course you do." He says something in Spanish and then in English. "I need to make a phone call. Help yourself to whatever you want or need." He leans in closer, over the bar. "What is mine is yours, Pri. What I do is for you. One day you'll understand that." And then to my surprise, he downs his drink, refills it, and walks up the stairs behind him.

Chapter Twenty-Eight

PRI

What I do is for you.
One day you'll understand that.
My God, it feels like he's saying goodbye, like I might go to sleep and wake up with him gone, never to be seen again. The idea guts me, truly hurts me on the deepest of levels. He's pushing me away, but these words don't speak of a man who doesn't love me. They speak of a man with a far more complicated agenda, a man who hates himself and what he's become.

This idea that he has to be willing to die or give up everything to repent, and I believe that's exactly where he's at right now, has to end now.

I down a big swallow of my drink, and with the burn still in my throat, round the bar in a sweeping move that has me hurrying up the stairs. I arrive at the top landing just in time to capture a glimpse of Adrian entering a doorway. I pursue him, my heart thundering in my chest, but nerves have never stopped me from facing a challenge and they won't stop me now.

I step into the doorway of a bedroom, with Adrian outside my visual range. An oversized but simple king-sized bed with a gray frame and cushioned headboard sits at the center wall. There are no pictures, no fancy furnishings. It's a clean, sleek, room. And the simplicity is somehow so very Adrian—a simple man on the surface, with a complicated story. To the right I find Adrian, his back to me, one hand pressed to a floor-to-ceiling window, a low-lying cloud black and heavy with rain, hovering in the sky, dimming the room—*his* room, his sanctuary even more so than the apartment and I know he knew I'd follow him here.

And the message is clear: If I want to see him and talk to him, I'll have to go to him.

I run my hands down my hips, still nervous. Why am I nervous? This is Adrian. I'm more comfortable with this man than I have ever been with another human being. The problem is he's not comfortable with himself. He hates himself. And he sees a future through that scope and no other. That thought, that certainty, inspires me to start moving toward him. He needs to see himself through my eyes. He needs it. *Really* needs it. And yet on some level, I am certain he brought me here, to this room, to finally, in his mind, show me the monster he sees in the mirror.

A dark energy radiates off of him, an unfamiliar energy that only seems to validate my assumption for why he's led me here to his room, to be that man he claims to be: dirty, bad, *wild*. In my world, knowledge is power, but that doesn't keep my heart from racing as I step toward him. And I swear there is a spike in his energy, as if, even without turning around, he knows I'm closing in on him. A short step leads me to the sitting area, where the couch is, to stand with my back to the window and facing him. But I don't touch him. And he doesn't touch me. "I'm here," I say. "With you. And I don't want to be anywhere else."

"Until you do."

It's such an Adrian response, I think. "Until I do?" I ask. "Is that what you assume every moment you're with me? And if I don't get there myself, as you expect, you'll get there for me? Is that what you did on the plane? Get there for me? Push me? Drive me away? Tell me I don't even know what love is or is not?" My anger is real, ripped from my heart, but unexpected and free in this moment. I don't hold back. I step even closer to him, so close we're almost touching. "I love you. I know I love you. You know I love you." I'm still not done, as I add, "But it would be oh so easy to walk away if I'd just hate you the way you hate yourself, now wouldn't it?"

"If I wanted to walk away, Pri, I'd walk away."

"Walking away is your entire plan. It was always your plan."

His hands come down on my waist, the heat of the touch scorching, spiking a charge between us. He backs me up, presses me to the steel bar dividing the window panes. "If I wanted to walk away, I'd walk away now and save myself. Everything I'm doing right now, from this point forward, is about saving you. Do what I'm telling you to do, Pri. Drop the case."

"No. You're not going to kill him. You didn't go there before. You're not going to start now."

A muscle in his jaw ticks. His hands fall from my sides, and press to the glass on either side of my head. "You don't know me."

He's said that too many times—so many times—but there's a difference to his tone this time, a finality, an acceptance of what comes next. He doesn't want to say more, he feels this time that he has no option. So I say just that. "Tell me," I urge softly. "And trust me to know the difference between the real you and the man who was undercover with Waters."

"And yet, you know nothing at all. That's why you need me."

My hand goes to his face and he catches my wrist, his dark eyes meeting mine, his words charging in ahead of mine. "I watched women get raped, let women suffer as sex slaves, stood by as men were murdered, beaten, and tortured. That's what you will hear in your depositions, in my testimony, Pri."

He releases me and then just stands there, staring at me, waiting for my judgment. Waiting for my shock and disgust that doesn't come. But these were no real confessions. The real confession is somewhere buried inside him, eating him alive, and it's about his brother, but my gut tells me not to push him in that direction. Not now, at least. "You think I don't know all of those things?"

"You know of them, yes. But it's the details, Pri. The devil is in the details."

"The devil is in your self-hate."

"The devil is in *me*." His voice is low but almost guttural with that insistence. And then he grabs my hands and presses them over my head, shackling them against the steel pillar, but the rest of his body doesn't touch me. "I've been gentle with you. I've protected you." He leans in, his cheek pressed to mine, lips at my ear. "Maybe that's the problem. You don't know what I'm capable of. You don't know who you're running from."

On some level, I know he's trying to scare me away, that he believes I will hate him, that it's inevitable, and the sooner the better. He believes hating him protects me. And suddenly I know that my hating him would be exactly what destroys him.

Heat rushes over me with the nearness of his body, with the promise of dark, erotic things to follow, that will surely test my limits, but this is Adrian. That statement to me says it all and I dare to whisper, "Show me."

He pulls back, his eyes lit with just a hint of surprise, as I add, "I'm not afraid of you."

Chapter Twenty-Nine

ADRIAN

I stare down at Pri, too beautiful, brave, and smart for her own good, and mine, too. She thinks she knows evil but seeing it from a distance, even a close distance, is not the same as living it.

There is a pulse in the air between us, a dark, demanding pulse that is more about me than her, but she doesn't see that. Because as smart as she is, and she is, she wears blinders with me. She simply can't see that there is a part of me that is far from gentle, a part of me that I discovered when I was a Devil. A part of me I can never fully erase.

I want to fuck her.

I want to fuck her so damn hard and right that she never wants to leave me.

But I don't think she can handle what that means. And if she can't handle that side of me, and if she can't handle *that* dark, hungry, far-from-gentle part of me, then she can't handle the rest of my story.

Any other time, that would be enough for me to pull back.

But not tonight. Tonight, I need her to understand everything is not roses and chocolates. It's fucking, just to get a high that makes you forget the blood and pain, and that is not even a little bit gentle. That's not lovemaking. That is grinding it out, roughing it up, until nothing exists but pleasure. And it's about control. It's about the world stripping it away and my need to claim it again, which is what I'm trying to do with Waters. But she isn't listening. She has to listen.

I now know that means no turning back. It means I need to show her how a Devil fucks.

"You trust me?" I challenge softly.

Her lips part and she whispers, "You know I do."

"Show me and I'll tell you anything you want."

"I've already shown you," she says. "You know I trust you."

She doesn't understand but she will. "Show me again," I say.

"All right," she says. "What do you want right now, Adrian? *Tell me.*"

Her. I want her for the rest of my life, but even above that, I want her alive and happy. Her life over my life. That's what this is about. The room darkens, the cloud just behind Pri outside the window is heavy with the promise of rain, ready to burst. An ominous reminder of how explosive and ready to burst our situation has become.

"Let's see how much you really do trust me, Pri," I say. "I'm in charge. You are not. You do as I say when I say it."

Her rebellion is instant. "And if I don't?"

"I'll punish you," I say, my voice absolute.

Her eyes go wide. "How?"

I leave that question unanswered. "Undress," I order softly.

I step backward and sit on the couch that faces the window, leaving two oversized—and perhaps useful before this is over—chairs free. I'm now in a position to watch her, to dominate her, and there is a flicker of uncertainty in her eyes that tells me she's aware of this fact. She's a woman who prefers control. Giving it away will not be easy for her. Giving it away is a sign of ultimate trust.

Her eyes narrow on me and for a moment I see rebellion, but then there's a softening of her expression that I know to be the first hints of submission. Only with Pri, I'm not sure it's actual submission. And while submission isn't what I want from Pri, not normally, not outside of the bedroom, at least there's a part of me that needs certain things.

She's going to meet that part of me now.

She chooses the least intimate move next. She toes off her shoes and then pulls off her socks. Her bare feet and pink painted toes draw my attention, and it seems my cock is alive and well, with the idea that more skin will soon follow. My gaze lifts to hers, a push in its depths. I expect her to push back, to hesitate again before removing her clothing, but she doesn't. She reaches for the hem of her T-shirt. The tee hits the floor and she gives me only a moment to appreciate her high, full breasts, cupped by the silk of the black bra before she's unhooked it and tossed it aside.

Her pretty pink nipples pucker with the cool air, and while I should be enjoying "the game" and this is a game we're playing, already I just want to grab her and pull her to me. But that's not what this night is about. I glance at her pants and then back to her face. "Everything," I order.

"What about you?"

I arch a brow. "What about me?"

"When are you going to undress?"

I fight the urge to promise her my protection, even now, when I'm the one making her feel vulnerable.

There's a growing part of me that wants what I want, and that's all of her, the parts of her that she shows no one. I also know that despite my reasons for taking her to that place tonight, for asking for that from her, it's not completely fair. Not when we both know I'm leaving. I have to leave.

She hesitates a minute longer, the room silent but for the sound of our breathing, and the heat of demand and vulnerability that almost hums. That's what I want. No music for distraction. No words. Just us. Just the anticipation of what comes next.

Pri shoves down her pants and panties at once and kicks them aside. My gaze rakes down her beautiful body and lingers in all the sweet spots as she says, "Now what?"

My eyes meet hers. "Get down on your knees."

Chapter Thirty

PRI

Get down on your knees.

That command by Adrian intimidates, and I expect it to stir uneasy, old demons that Logan created, but it doesn't. There is just that intimate arousal. I am so turned on that my sex aches and my breasts are heavy.

Adrian won't hurt me. Adrian won't force anything on me that I don't want to do. I know this, deep in my core. I know this.

And I also know that he doesn't really believe I trust him enough to be this vulnerable with him. He believes I'll prove him right, but I also think he wants me to prove him wrong.

And I already have.

I love this man.

I go down on my knees.

Chapter Thirty-One

ADRIAN

Pri doesn't just go down on her knees.

She does so right in front of me and her hands settle on my thighs.

Her naked, with her hands on my body, is about the end of me and this game, but this is bigger than the moment. I need her to understand that no matter what good she brings out in me, there are other parts of me, darker parts of me, that will not go away. Parts she won't like. Once she understands that, her thinking will shift.

I remove her hands. "Touch me when I tell you to touch me."

"But I *want* to touch you."

"And I want you to touch me. Just not yet. Trust, Pri. I'm in control. You do what I say."

"And if I don't?"

"I'll punish you."

"Punish me?" she challenges. "Is that supposed to scare me, Adrian?"

She thinks I can't challenge her. She's wrong. "Hands and knees, Pri. Right here in front of me."

Her teeth worry her bottom lip and there is a flicker of apprehension in her eyes before she gives a small laugh that is really not a laugh at all. Her lashes lower and then lift as she says, "All right then," she says. "I will."

She rotates slightly and settles on her hands and knees. My cock throbs with the sight of her, naked and submissive. My hand settles on her back, between her shoulder blades. "Don't move. Okay?"

"Yes."

I push to my feet and undress, my skin hot, my cock so damn hard it hurts. When my clothes are set aside, I sit back down on the couch, and my hand returns to her back. "Now what?" she asks.

"Now this," I say, running my hand down her spine, my mouth replacing my hand between her shoulder blades, my tongue teasing the delicate skin. She arches her back and my hand travels to her backside and gives it a squeeze. My other hand is on her belly, sliding low, and when I give her a tiny pat, just enough to shock her, she gasps, but my fingers are already sliding between her thighs. I go down on my knee beside her, and when I give her a full-palm squeeze, I say, "We'll stop if you want to stop. Just say the word."

She glances back at me, her eyes heavy and whispers, "I know that, Adrian."

Because she trusts me. And I want her to trust me. Suddenly, I don't know what the hell I'm trying to do right now. I don't want her to distrust me. I don't want her to hate me. But she will, I remind myself. She will when she knows the devil in the details—unless she doesn't.

Suddenly, I have a flashback to being on the com when she was fighting off Logan and I really don't know what the hell I'm doing. Fuck. I grab Pri and pull her around to me, fingers in her hair, my hand molding her close. "I'm sorry. So damn sorry."

"Sorry? What are you blaming yourself for now?"

"Logan all but raped you, Pri, and you haven't even had a chance to deal with that. And what the hell do I do? Pull this power play on you."

"So I'm not supposed to be enjoying this?" She catches my arm and pulls my hand around, pressing my fingers between her thighs, and gasping as she does. "Because I am."

And she is. Wet. Hot. Temptation from the moment I met her. "God, woman," I murmur, and then my mouth slants over her mouth, and our tongues collide. And right now, I don't give a shit about games and hate or what comes next. I just want Pri.

My fingers slide inside her and she moans into my mouth, arching against my hand. There is no distrust in her, she's all here, in full abandonment mode, melting against my hand. Melting into my body. I lift her and us to the couch, dragging her with me, and then she's straddling me, and we're pressed close, our mouths, our bodies.

"I need inside you," I whisper.

And she replies with, "God yes. Now. Please."

If I wasn't hard already, her "God yes. Now. Please." would have done the job. I catch her waist, anchor her hips and then, Lord help me, her hand is on my cock, guiding it to her sex. She presses me inside her and slowly slides down my erection, too damn slowly. I pull her down on top of me and drag her forward, feel the squeeze as I bring her lips to my lips. And right there, breathing with her, I forgot every plan I had to push her away.

I just want her closer.

I arch into her, thrusting. She presses against me and then we're not kissing. We're moving together, watching each other as we do. She pushes off of my shoulders, sitting there, naked and beautiful, her breasts swaying with our movements. One minute it's this slow dance of our bodies and then next, my hand is on her breast, fingers pinching her nipple and she is nipping my lips with her teeth. We're wild then, this crazy, wild ride of need and lust, and there is nothing else but us.

When she buries her face in my neck and says, "Adrian," almost desperately, it's the prelude to the spasm of her sex around my cock. I groan with the intensity of that moment and then I'm grinding into release. We shudder and shake together and when she collapses on top of me, I roll her over, her back to the couch, leaning over her.

And I tell her exactly what I feel. "What I said on the plane was bullshit. I was just trying to protect you."

Her hand presses to my face. "I know you want to protect me. But maybe it's better if we protect each other, together, you know?"

Together.

That word is so unfamiliar and yet so right with Pri.

"I love you, Pri. And that's why I don't like what that means for you."

"I don't want to be here without you. I will go anywhere with you, Adrian."

That statement is a loaded one. More than she knows. Because where I go doesn't erase the danger. I'm a walking target and so is she unless I end this. And that's a reality I have to make her face. There's no hiding from this.

The devil is on our doorstep.

Chapter Thirty-Two

PRI

I will go anywhere with you, Adrian.

I see the torment in Adrian's face over my words, but it's not about him pushing me away, as my insecurity had me fearing after the airplane incident. He just simply doesn't believe there is only one way out of this outside of him letting Waters drag him to hell with him. Adrian wants to protect me. He proves that over and over, as he just did when he worried about me being affected by what happened with Logan.

I press my hand to his face and say, "You are not the devil you think you are," saving him a reply. "Now feed me that grand pizza you promised. I'm actually starving."

"Pizza wins the moment," he says, but he doesn't move. "Pri—"

"I know," I say softly. "Just—feed me."

He hesitates, and says, "There are things I need to say to you, but clothes and food, then conversation."

"Yes," I say. "Clothes, food, conversation."

He pushes off of me and stands, helping me up. We dress in comfortable silence and when the clouds reach their limit and burst with an explosion of rain, the two of us step to the window, staring into the storm.

Lightning flickers left and right and Adrian pulls me in front of him. For a long time, we stay right there. Me and him. The two of us above the world, or at least the city, and just out of reach of the storm.

"We'll figure it out," he says, turning me to face him. "*Together*." He strokes a lock of hair behind my ear. "You and me, Pri." I want to ask if that means he's decided against his crazy plan, but for some reason, it feels like the wrong time. He cups my hand and kisses my knuckles. "Let's order that pizza. And I have some wine you might like over that whiskey."

"Wine would be nice. Can we stay up here?"

"Yes. Let's stay up here." He snakes his phone from his pocket. "I'll order."

"I'm going to the bathroom."

He nods and I walk into the bedroom, and past the bed to the open doors on the other side of the room. Flipping on the light, I find stone floors and brown stone counters with flecks of tile here and there in brown and white accents. Everything about this place is unique and custom-designed, and I'm curious why someone who didn't plan to stay around created something that says otherwise.

I quickly do what I need to do and return to the bedroom. Adrian is at the window, talking on the phone. Curious about any updates, I close the space between us, and the minute he sees me, I don't miss the warmth that floods his eyes. Or the warmth that floods my body. I had no idea it was possible to react to another human being as I do Adrian.

"Keep me posted," he says to the person on the line. "Right. Later." He disconnects and points to the bottle of wine that's on a stone table that was not sitting there earlier, but rather to the side by a chair.

He sits down on the couch and I join him, watching him fill our glasses, the rain a steady thrum on the window, low thunder humming in the not-so-distant distance.

"Is everything okay?" I ask. "The call. Was that Blake?"

"It was," he confirms. "And all is quiet."

"Is it safe to order pizza?"

"I have a delivery booth. They leave the food. It comes up a dumbwaiter."

"You're kidding me."

"I am not." He hands me a glass. "I built this place with everything in mind. And with a lot of help from Walker."

"But you always planned to leave."

"I didn't plan to leave, Pri. I prepared to leave. There's a difference." He sips the wine. "Do you like it?"

I try it, letting the sweet berries touch my tongue. "It's good," I say. "Sweet, the way I like it." My mind starts racing with all the unanswered questions plaguing our situation. "Is there any word on my parents? Or rather, did my mother accept protection?"

"She did not," he says. "But if your father is as dirty as we think, at least for now, she's safe."

"But I go back to that message Logan left me. He told me he's been protecting me more than I know. He also said I'd find out what that meant."

"And you still don't have any idea?"

"No, but it feels like some sort of ticking bomb, about to go off. What if it's about my parents? It feels like that's the only thing it could be. Like he plans to blame my family for some sin of his own."

"We'll figure it out and handle it. Believe it or not, it's already seven o'clock. We're all tired. We need to lay low for now. The team will ensure we're clear tomorrow and then gather here, where we'll spend a few hours with them planning for what comes next."

"That's what you decided on the phone?"

"Yes. That's pretty much all, too, Pri. There are no secrets."

A buzzer goes off. "The pizza place is right across the street," he says, his fingers brushing my cheek before he says, "Secrets don't work. I see that now." And then he gets up and walks away.

I stand up and watch him disappear out of the door and then turn to the wide windows and spot a long streak of lightning across the sky. *Secrets don't work. I see that now.* He has a new plan to make me hate him. He's going to introduce me to the devil he sees in the mirror. The one that doesn't exist.

Chapter Thirty-Three

ADRIAN

I hit the recall button on the dumbwaiter and while it hums with movement, I press my hands to the wall on either side, Savage's words in my head, the bastard. Savage talking about leaving the woman he loved behind to save her: *"I tried to fuck her out of my system. I took jobs I was certain would get me killed. I liked that idea. I drank too much. I did all the standard miserable loser things I could do. None of it worked. And the fucked-up part? The enemy found her anyway."*

The dumbwaiter buzzes its arrival and I hit the button to open the door, the delicious smell of baked bread and tomato sauce unable to distract me from my thoughts. I'm back in that conversation with Savage: *"Eventually you have to tell Pri if you want the two of you to work."*

I don't have that option, I think, but damn it, even when Waters is gone, will Deleon live, and go after Pri? Will one of the others inside the Devils?

"Damn it," I murmur, grabbing the pizzas and shutting the door. I start walking and it's as if Savage is here, answering me again: *"Truth be told, maybe Pri can't handle the truth, but you have to tell her anyway.*

And truth be told, maybe it's not the right time. Maybe she has a hero complex right now for you. Make sure it's real before you tell her. I don't know what is real shit or not for you two, but hear this and hear it well. Don't assume walking away from her is the best way to love her. That's you fucking up."

I find myself at the bar, setting down the pizzas. And then behind the bar, pouring a drink. "This is me fucking up," I murmur, downing the drink and refilling it before walking to the window, darkness, and rain in view.

I sit down on the coffee table and squeeze my eyes shut, my mind traveling back to the past, back to a night with Waters.

Waters is at the head of the war room table with me and Deleon on his left and right. No one else is present. Ricki Lenerd, Waters' attorney at the time, is here by emergency request. He stands at the end of the table, dressed in an expensive suit, his face freshly shaven, his green eyes sharp but worried. He's forty-five, bald, and used his mid-life crisis and the money Waters paid him to land a twenty-five-year-old wife too pretty for the likes of him.

"Sit," Waters orders.

Lenerd hesitates, uncomfortable in an obvious way but he sits down next to me and blurts out, "I'm officially resigning as your attorney."

The resignation really isn't a surprise to me. Several missing women, connections to Waters, and bad press have created unease in Lenerd. I'd say he was a smart man on that point, but he's not. He wanted money. He went down this path. He won't just walk away. Even before Waters speaks, I know Lenerd is about to get a rude awakening.

Waters smirks, amused and irritated at the same time. "I don't accept your resignation. You're a lifetime, Ricki my boy. The money I've loaded into your bank account says so. That pretty red sports car your wife drives says so." He leans forward. "I say so."

"I'm not the right man for this job, not anymore." He reaches into his briefcase and sets a thick envelope on the table. "A hundred thousand dollars to buy my freedom."

He motions to Deleon and Deleon takes the envelope and checks the contents. "About right," he confirms.

"Well then," Waters says. "We have a deal, Ricki boy." He gives him a moment to feel relief, watches his shoulders relax before he adds, "Your pretty little wife with those fuck me blue eyes and long legs can keep fucking you instead of me. At least for now."

Thunder rumbles loudly, shaking the walls and dragging me back to the present, where I'd much rather live. I down my drink, dispose of my glass on the table and walk to the window. And I do so with an understanding I should have had from the beginning with Pri. She's connected to me. With Waters and Deleon dead, she will probably be safe, but I can't be sure. And I'm not trusting anyone else to protect her. Am I making an excuse to keep her with me? Maybe. But I'm done thinking she's better off without me. That ship has sailed.

"Adrian."

Pri says my name a moment before she steps between me and the glass. She doesn't speak and I cup her head and pull it to mine, drawing a deep breath before I look down at her. "If we're doing this, baby, you and me, you need to know the things I did when I was with Waters. You need to know about my brother."

Her hands flatten on my chest. "When you're ready—"

"I will never be ready, but that doesn't change the fact that you need to know. I didn't want to kill him. I was trying to save him." I release her and grab my glass, walking back to the bar. I need to be drunk for this, despite the fact that I know logically that I didn't commit a crime. Maybe not in the eyes of the law, but in the eyes of God and family, that's another story.

I round the bar and fill a glass. Pri joins me on the other side of the counter, and I fill a glass and push it toward her. "We both need to drink."

"I think you're blowing this up into something it's not, Adrian. Did you kill him in cold blood?"

"No. Fuck no. I loved him, but the truth is, Pri, he had a bad side none of us understood. Like we needed to save him from himself."

"Us? Who is us?"

"Me and Raf. When Raf was eighteen, he had a girlfriend. We left her at the house and went out to the firing range. We came back and she was sitting on the porch. It was raining and cold. She ran to Raf and wrapped her arms around him and started to cry. Alex was there. And he had pushed himself on her."

"Oh my God. What did Rafael do?"

"They fought. And it wasn't good for Raf. He's not the beast, Alex was, but he was pissed and he fought with all he had."

"Why do I know that it did not end well?"

"Because it didn't." I scrub my jaw, back in the past for a moment. "Raf made me promise to let him fight his own battles. I let it go on too long before I just couldn't take it. I pulled Alex off of him, but he was bad, really bad, Pri. Twenty stitches, his eyes swollen shut, and a concussion, bad."

"And Alex?"

"I beat the shit out of him, while Raf's girlfriend rushed him to the hospital. Dad came home and pulled me off of him—too soon if you want to know the truth."

"What did your father say?"

"That he'd handle it. And I know he tried. That man loved us. The problem was he was gone too much, and Mom just couldn't control Alex."

"The idea of Alex in law enforcement is not a good one," Pri says, sipping her drink. "I know cops with a personality I could see behaving like Alex when the right people aren't looking."

"Yes well, me too, unfortunately. I never thought it was a good idea. Dad thought it was his ticket to being right and good. I thought it would become about power to Alex."

"Did it?"

"We didn't work together, but I heard stories. And I damn sure didn't want him going undercover with the Devils. He was corruptible. I knew that."

"And you were right," she says.

"They brought out that part of him that went after Raf's girlfriend and then beat the shit out of Raf."

She leans in closer, her hand covering mine where it holds my glass. "Tell me," she urges softly.

LISA RENEE JONES

166

Chapter Thirty-Four

ADRIAN

Tell me.

Pri's words burn inside me. Simple words that don't feel simple at all.

I tell myself to just stand here and tell Pri about Alex. I tell myself that words are simple. I'm just telling a story. I refill my glass and then ignore it. I need to stop drinking and stay clear-minded for about ten reasons, one of which is that this is serious business. And she matters too damn much to me for me to haze my way through it. Adrenaline surges and I round the bar and walk to the living room, standing at the window again, thinking about that deadly night when Alex became my enemy.

I'm aware of Pri inching closer and sitting on the table, perhaps exactly where I had been minutes before. Waiting on me, but not pushing. Thunder roars and lightning shoots in three directions across the sky. The lights flicker and turn off, the entire block shrouded in darkness, and Pri's soft gasp has my attention. I turn and she is on her feet, and even as I reach for her, she falls into my arms. The generator groans to life and the lights turn back on.

"Please tell me that was the storm."

"It was and is," I promise, stroking her hair and pulling her around in front of me to the window, showing her the dark city that assures her we're not alone.

I step behind her, my hand settling on her belly. "We're the lucky ones with a generator," I say, kissing her neck. "We're safe. You're safe with me, Pri."

She flattens her hand on my hand on her belly and says, "And you're safe with me."

My eyes lower with the punch of her words. *I'm safe with her.* I can trust her, I know I can—I do, but it's not about trust. And the truth is that she will understand why I killed Alex. She won't understand how I handled it after the fact. And that's the segue to all the shit I had to just "let" happen with Waters.

She squeezes my hand but doesn't turn around, almost as if she knows I need the shelter of her looking at the city, not at me. It's as if she is once again saying, you're safe with me, and that undoes my reserve.

"There was a woman," I begin, and when I feel her stiffen slightly I add, "Not my woman. Not a woman I even knew. A woman."

The tension eases from her body, at least for the moment, as I continue. "We were at the clubhouse, and there was a big party. There was always a party. I'm talking massive, though. Bikes everywhere, Devils in from all over the country. A bonfire. Booze. Drugs. And women. Lots of women. There were also tents, tipi style, expensive monster tents that Waters called sex caves. Most of the action was there, outside around the fire and inside the tents. I went inside the clubhouse to take a piss. Alex was already there."

I wrap my arms around Pri and bury my face in her neck, some part of me holding onto her to stay here in the present but it's too late. The memory is here, corrosive, punching at me, pulling me back. And suddenly, I'm living that night all over again.

I walk in the back door of the clubhouse and thank fuck it's quiet. The game I'm playing every second of my life is taking a toll. When I walk back outside, I have to drink and smack asses and pretend like I'm one of them, while plotting shit that I should be arresting them for instead of helping them. I step into the hall bathroom, relieve myself, and splash water on my face before looking in the mirror and whispering, "You will not kill Waters. That's not the answer." Yet more and more, I'm not sure if that's true. And I still have no proof he killed Mom and Dad. If I had it, he probably would be dead.

I exit the bathroom and a woman's voice lifts. "No. No. Stop. Stop it."

I curse under my breath because I'm not watching anyone get raped today. That shit is not on today's agenda. Anger that has built over months at this outlaw group and its leaders drives me forward and around the corner. The voice lifts again. "No. Ouch. Stop it. Stop."

The voice is coming from the war room and I shove open the door to find Alex all over some woman, and just in time to watch him rip down her top, and expose her breasts. She slaps him and he catches her hand. "Bitch," he growls.

"What the fuck are you doing, Alex?" I demand, my voice low, brittle. I cannot even believe what I'm seeing right now, but then, I should. More and more, he's become one of them, one of the Devils.

He squeezes the woman's breast and flicks her nipple. "What does it look like I'm doing?"

She squirms in his arms and he elbows her in the face, her head jerking left.

"Let her go," I order.

"When I'm done with her, I will," he says, "but I'm not even close to done. Go back to the party."

"What would Dad say right now, Alex?"

"Fuck off, Adrian. I'm sick of your high horse bullshit."

The woman recovers from the elbow and explodes on him, punches at him, squirming and sobbing. He laughs and yanks her off the table to turn her and force her to lay on top of it, yanking her skirt up. I grab him and yank him off of her. She whirls on him and punches again, but he grabs her by the hair and twists it around his hand. She screams with the pain of it. I knock the shit out of him and he lets her go.

He puffs up and scowls at me. "What are you doing, Adrian?"

"This isn't who we are, Alex. Don't let this shit life change you."

The woman screams and flings herself at Alex, biting at him and clawing. He whirls on her, cursing in Spanish and flinging her off of him. She hits the table and bounces, her head smashing into the corner and there is a jerk of her neck. I know before she ever hits the ground this is bad, really fucking bad.

Fuck Waters and what he'll have to say about it. I reach for my phone to call for help.

Alex pulls his gun and points it at me. "Don't even think about it. Walk away, Adrian."

"I'm not going to do that. I'm calling an ambulance."

His eyes bore into me and his finger twitches on the trigger. "What are we doing, Alex?"

"He didn't kill Mom and Dad. It's time for you to walk away."

"I'm not going anywhere. Not without you."

The woman moans, and he growls in irritation, turning toward her, and to my complete shock, he shoots her. He turns back toward me and it's in his eyes. That intent and I have to make a split-second decision—live or die. Adrenaline surges and I fire. He fires as well, but my bullet hits first, and his hand moves, his shot zooming past my head. A second later, he hits the ground.

Waters walks into the room, glances at the scene, and then at me. "Clean it up," is all he says, and he disappears out of the room.

I blink back to the present, still holding Pri, and I tell her everything. And then I wait for her reaction.

LISA RENEE JONES

Chapter Thirty-Five

ADRIAN

Pri turns in my arms and presses her hands to my face. "How could you think I would hate you for this? *How?* You did nothing wrong." Her voice is raw, rasping with emotion.

"Aside from trying to save a woman I got killed?" I ask bitterly. "Aside from the fact, there were others I didn't even try and save. I couldn't or I would have ended up dead."

"You did your job. And you didn't get her killed. Your brother was crazy."

"I shot him in the heart, Pri." Now my voice is raspy, my throat burning with acid. "It was instinct. Shoot to kill. I get that. I get that it happened so *damn fast*. But I could have shot him somewhere else."

She wraps her arms around me. "A split-second decision," she says. "He pulled the trigger. Had you taken one more second, you'd be dead, not him."

"He was my brother. *My brother.*" Those last two words are torn from the very core of me.

"I know," she says, her hands pressed to my chest. "I know. But he would have killed you. Why didn't you tell the FBI what happened? What did you tell them?"

"That he disappeared. That's all I told them."

"Why?" she asks, confusion in her voice, a slight lift in her tone. "Why not tell the truth?"

"He's my brother, Pri."

Her head tilts and her eyes narrow a moment before she says, "You don't want them to know he was dirty."

I give a short nod. "Right now," I say, "he's a hero, just like Dad." I cup her face. "Do not tell anyone. You are the only one who knows. You are the only one I've told."

"I won't. You know I won't." She tears up. "I can't believe you've carried this burden alone. You're safe with me, remember?"

God, I love this woman, and I thumb away her tears. "I haven't told Rafael. I have to tell him. I know that."

"Yes," she agrees. "I think you do, but when the time is right. Now is not that time. He won't hate you, I promise you. Just like I could never hate you. I love you, Adrian."

"I love you, too, Pri, but you need to hear it all." I stroke another tear from her cheek. "I need to tell you everything. And no matter what decision is made about how we handle Waters, my testimony needs to be on file. I want you to take my deposition. Now. Tonight. I have the equipment."

"And if I don't hate you after?" she challenges.

"We'll talk about it after."

Chapter Thirty-Six

PRI

Somehow the storm that just won't end seems an extension of Adrian.

Thanks to his fancy generator, we heat the pizza and manage to talk about things other than Alex and Waters. I get him to tell me about Rafael's success and he perks up. "He was always singing and dancing," he says. "And damn good at it. Which is why he always had the ladies at his heels."

"Does he have a special lady now?"

"I don't know," he says. "If we find a way out of this, we'll surprise him and show up to a concert, and then afterward, I'll find out what he's really up to when he's not on the stage."

If we find a way out of this. He means when he kills Waters. I try not to think about that reality. I tell myself there's another way. The problem is he's not wrong about anything he's said. Waters will remain powerful, even behind bars. I don't know how we fix that. It feels like a conversation I should want to have with Ed, but funny thing is that I haven't thought about Ed at all these past twenty-four hours. "Is Ed here in New York?" I ask, finishing off a second slice of delicious pizza, while Adrian is on about his sixth. "He is, right?"

175

"He's staying in one of the safe houses," he says, "but honestly, I haven't gotten an update on what the team thinks about him. We'll update you on everything tomorrow."

I nod, and sip the bottle of water I'm drinking, but Ed is on my mind and bothering me.

He's the DA. He's handled high-profile cases. He should have been more prepared for how out of control this case has become. Why wasn't he? Is he incompetent? Or was it intentional? I think about my connection to my father, and how I was moved to lead on this case. If my father is dirty, and Ed is dirty, what if—God. I glance at Adrian. "What if my father and Ed are dirty? Adrian, what if I was put on the case because my father promised he could control me?"

He set his plate aside. "I want to tell you your father isn't involved, Pri. You now know just how much I understand how much you want your father to be a good man. But I won't be anything but honest with you."

"It's possible," I say. "It's more than possible."

"It is," he agrees. "But you didn't let your father control you. And that's a good thing."

"A good thing that feels like it's going to end badly."

"Not if we can help it," he promises.

But some things can't be helped, I add silently. Or stopped. As Alex proved when he fired on Adrian. And in some ways, I feel like that's exactly what my father did to me in that restaurant.

Adrian sets up the recording equipment in a library. The furnishings are gray leather, accented with fluffy gray rugs, and walls lined with books that range from fiction to history, medical and legal journals, and then some.

"You never know when a random fact will save your life," he explains, sitting down on the leather couch, with me beside him.

Thanks to the Walker team, I have at least some of my clothes and all of my work supplies. I pull out a list of questions I've long worked on for the day I interviewed Adrian Mack. And so, I begin. I start with the basics, with his name, work history, family life. Then I move to his career and we eventually dive into his time with Waters. From there, hours in, and two breaks later, we start talking about the crimes I want him to detail.

And in most cases, he can, and does, holding nothing back about what he saw and when he saw it. He was right. He saw murder. He saw rape. He saw horrible beatings. Not to mention theft and drug crimes. Each time he describes the torment of watching, of trying to find a way to help that would not get him killed.

When I'm about to end the recording, he says, "Ask me about Deleon."

Another two hours, later I turn off the recording device, cold and numb. Adrian and I stare at each other, and I can see the torment in his eyes. These things he saw and lived will haunt him for a lifetime. I know this. And I understand—God, I understand so many things.

I stand up and step in front of him. He doesn't touch me but when our eyes meet, his self-hate is like hell blazing in his stare, all but overtaking the good man he can't see anymore. I press my hands to his face.

"Good thing I love you more than you hate yourself."

The heat of his self-hate dims, banked for a moment as his expression softens and his hands settle on my hips. "Pri, baby. I don't—"

"But I do," I say. "To whatever you were going to say. And I know now why you want to kill Waters. But just promise, promise me we'll try to find another way. And don't tell me there isn't another way. Not tonight."

He draws a deep breath and pushes to his feet, and now he's cupping my face. "Not tonight," he promises, and then he kisses me, scoops me up, and carries me to his bedroom.

Chapter Thirty-Seven

PRI

Well after midnight, I'm snuggled into Adrian's bed with him after eating way too many M & M's which I'm quickly learning is the man's weakness, while he is mine. He swears I'm his, but as my lashes lower and his hot, hard body holds me close, I believe that's the problem. I'm his weakness, and Waters knows it. In a groggy moment, I wonder how we can use that against Waters, but I drift into slumber.

I wake to the patter of rain on the window, with bad weather that clearly has not passed, and Adrian missing. A glance at the clock indicates it's after nine, and I should have long been out of bed. Throwing away the blankets, I reach for my phone to find a note from Adrian:

Hot coffee and hotter Latin man downstairs waiting on you.

I laugh and set the note aside to check my phone and find three messages. The first is from my mother. I hit the play button: *Please, just do as your father asks. He has his reasons. One of which is to keep us safe. I need you to trust me on this, honey. Do this for me.*

A stab of disappointment rips through me at her obvious involvement in whatever Father is doing, be it by way of pretending obliviousness or otherwise. Ignorance is still guilt, but my mind travels back to the dinner we'd shared. She'd rushed into the restaurant in disarray. She is never in disarray. It was clear from the moment she sat down she was not herself. I slip back into the memory.

"Let's order food. I need to eat something. I feel shaky. And let's get some of that yummy bread."

"Okay," I say. "Yes. I know what you like. I can order." I wave at the waitress, place our order, and we have bread pronto.

She quickly butters a slice and I do the same. "How are you?" she asks.

"I'm okay. You are not. What is happening?"

"I don't know. I mean, I do know. I thought your father was cheating on me."

"Oh. No. Tell me no."

"I did," she says. "I've spent a few weeks fretting over it. It's a big part of why I didn't leave the country. He urged me to go."

"You said—"

"I know what I said, but what was I going to say, Pri? I think your dad found a younger woman and I'm a washed-up old lady to him? It hurt, you know?"

"Of course it did, but you say it as if it's past tense?"

"Right well, I don't think he's cheating anymore. I'm actually thinking Italy sounds nice. Tuscany, maybe. Somewhere remote that I can just clear my head."

Snapping back to the present, something strikes me as odd. She thought he was cheating, but she didn't want to get away. That doesn't seem like a natural reaction. And yet, she declined protection and wants me to drop the case. But then again, she did do a one-eighty in that conversation. I think back to the dinner once more.

"Is Dad involved with Waters, Mom?"

She slides her plate away. "While snooping over the assumed affair, I overhead some things. That's why I wanted to meet here. I'm afraid our house is bugged."

"What things?" I ask, trying not to sound as urgent as the thundering of my heart suggests I am.

"Somehow, I suspect through Logan, your father got involved with Waters and is now trapped, held captive by that monster's demands. He can't get out and basically, Pri, honey, if you don't drop the case, they're going to implicate us all and send us to jail."

My eyes go wide and the room spins. "What? No. How do you know that?"

"I recorded a meeting your father had with some man I don't know. Your father never said his name, but he made it clear he didn't even know Waters was a client. The other man made it clear that the firm had laundered money for Waters for years now. Your father's implicated." She slides a tape recorder over to me. "Listen to it and drop the case, Pri."

Blood rushes in my ears. "I think you need to leave the country."

"I don't need to leave the country if you drop the case."

"And then what? Waters continues to control us if we don't stop him?"

"Maybe not," she says. "Maybe he'll move on."

"Move on? No, Mother. You're not being realistic. It's just a matter of time before he threatens us again."

"I told you," she snaps. "The man on the recording told your father that if you drop out of the case, Waters will free your father."

"Until he's not free," I say. "I'm going to get you on a plane out of the country in the morning. Pack a bag. I'll be by to pick you up."

"Dad—"

"Do not call him and tell him, Mom. The wrong people will find out. I'll tell him when he returns and try to get him to go and meet you. Okay?"

"I can't leave you and him here. I can't. What if something happens to you? If you two go, I'll go."

"Damn it, Mom."

"Drop the case, Pri." She motions to the waitress. "We need to-go boxes, please."

I squeeze my eyes shut against that memory. Yes, my father is being blackmailed, but only because he was already in the sewer with Waters. I'd like to think Logan got him into this, but for all I know, the opposite might be true.

I fear the family I knew is now the family I never knew at all. Family is supposed to stick together, but how do you stick with those who are doing bad things?

I think back to Adrian's torment over his brother and I understand all too well how he felt. He wanted to protect Alex, even when Alex didn't deserve his protection. That almost got him killed. I want to protect my family as well when they don't deserve it. Not at all. In fact, I have this horrible feeling that my father would choose Waters over me. That perhaps he already has.

In my mind's eye, I see me and my father, holding guns on each other. If it came down to it, who would pull the trigger first?

Will it come down to just that? Has it already?

Chapter Thirty-Eight

PRI

For the moment, I force myself to refocus on my phone, not the daunting task of a war with Waters.

I refocus on my message, and the next one is from Ed: *We need to talk. Call me.* I frown. I also don't call him back. I want to hear what Adrian and Blake have to say about him first.

I glance at the final message, which is from Grace. She works for the DA's offices, yes, but she's also a friend who is dating Josh, who we believe might be dirty. He might have left the DA's office for a private security company, but he showed up at the office and inserted himself into this case when he was never hired to help, which sits wrong. I quickly hit the play button to listen to the message: *Pri, what is going on? Everyone is talking about you and Ed being in protective custody. Well, except Cindy, who won't call me back.*

Cindy's an ADA on the case, working beneath me.

Grace continues: *The press showed up at my house this morning. I need you to call me. Please. How did they get to my house?*

I dial Blake and he answers on the first ring. "You're calling about Grace," he answers, confirming he's still monitoring my call, which is actually, right about now, comforting.

"Yes. How did the press get to her house?"

"Josh called them. We don't think Grace knows that piece of the puzzle."

I blanch. "What? Why? Why would he do that?"

"When she was swarmed, he took control, and name-dropped the new security company he's working for."

"Now I'm worried," I say. "You know she talked to Lucifer, right? She told him she thought Josh was dirty. I know her. She's sweet. She won't know how to break up with him if he's overwhelming her, not if she's afraid of him."

"Lucifer stayed behind in Austin last-minute for that very reason. He's going to be at the office, running things at your direction, and watching out for Grace."

"Oh," I say. "That's good. But can you tell him not to get her naked and stuff like that? She's vulnerable right now."

He laughs. "I'll certainly tell him not to get her naked and stuff. More later. I'll be there soon." He disconnects.

I glance up to find Adrian standing in the doorway, wearing nothing but low-slung sweatpants. His abs are distracting as is the cup of steaming coffee in his hand that makes this moment as perfect as it can be considering everything. This man, coffee, and the rest of my life, yes, please.

"You heard about Grace," he says, crossing to sit down next to me and offering me the steaming cup.

"I did and I'm worried. I have to call her. What do I say? What if she starts talking about Josh?"

"Blake had Ed call her for that reason. It's handled, at least for now. You can call her once we talk things out with Blake."

"*For now* seems to be the story of my life," I say, worried, but still in need of the coffee he's handed me. I sip from the cup to find a brew that is extra wonderful. "Is this chocolate?"

"It is. I like my coffee as close to my candy as possible."

I smile but it fades quickly. "Ed called me. Should I call him back?"

"I think you should shower and get ready before the team arrives. We need to talk through exactly who is a player on what team before you do anything."

"Which reminds me. My mother called. Did you hear the message?"

"No. Blake listens in. I prefer you to tell me what you want me to hear."

"I have nothing to hide."

He strokes hair behind my ear. "And neither do I anymore. You know that, right?"

"Not yet. Not until you decide to go rogue and kill Waters."

"I wouldn't exactly be going rogue," he reminds me. "You'd have to drop the case for us to have any hope that it won't go to trial."

"Ed could drop it," I say. "And some part of me worries he will. I have a bad feeling about him. Then Waters would be free and you could kill him. And then, then—I don't know." I cut my stare from his, suddenly aware that I don't know where I stand with Adrian. I love him. He loves me. But I think he's still leaving. I set my cup down and stand.

Adrian catches my hand and walks me between his legs. "Go with me."

I blink. "What?"

"I didn't want you to have to leave. I wanted you to stay alive. I didn't want to be the reason you had to leave, but now—"

"Now what's changed?" I ask, tension crawling up my spine. "Why are you suddenly—"

"No." He wraps his arm around my waist and scoops me closer. "Not suddenly. God no, Pri. I love you, woman."

"But you suddenly—"

"Nothing is sudden. Savage talked to me on the plane. He told me he left his wife, before they were married, to protect her. His enemies still found her. And they were both miserable apart. I'll be miserable without you, Pri. I'm hoping you feel the same way, but before you answer, know you have options."

The bliss of his misery without me is dashed quickly with unease. "Options? What does that mean?"

"I want you to come with me because you want to be with me, Pri. If you choose to stay, I've talked to Blake. Walker will offer you protection here in New York, in Texas, or somewhere else, based on your safety needs and comfort level. But just so you know, Blake is also going to offer you a job if you want it. If you accept, the pay is good, and you can work for him here or anywhere in the world. I want you to be happy and—"

"Which option are you?" I ask, tuning out the rest before he'd gotten very far at all. "A or B?"

His eyes narrow, apprehension in their depths. "A, Pri. I'm option A."

"Then A," I say. "I choose option A. And can you kiss me already?"

He drags me down to the bed and settles me under him, the delicious weight of him on top of me, his mouth closing down on mine. And for just a little while, with rain pelting the windows, we escape, just me and him. And there is a shift between us, a passion that is deeper, richer, warmer in ways that have nothing to do with our naked bodies. We've made a commitment to each other and no one, not even the Devil himself, can take that from us. We won't let him.

Chapter Thirty-Nine

PRI

Adrian and I shower and dress, and with a limited wardrobe, I end up once again in black jeans and a black T-shirt, but they are at least clean. Adrian dresses in distressed jeans, and a blue AC/DC T-shirt, paired with boots, and he's freshly shaved, aside from his neatly trimmed goatee. He looks good, relaxed even, but his mood is somehow a mix of light and dark. And I get it. He's unburdened after our talk last night to some degree, but he's still on edge, and how can he not be? We're in a bubble, in his apartment, but nothing has changed in the outside world. We are still hunted.

And as much as I disagree with freeing Waters so Adrian can kill him, more and more I understand that Waters is not even slightly under control. And more and more, I realize that I don't have an answer to fix that problem.

Adrian and I have breakfast delivered as his kitchen is not stocked, at least not with perishable items, and we choose egg-white omelets and fruit. We settle into comfortable conversation, and he tells me all about designing the apartment. We're almost done with our meal when my cellphone rings with Ed's number on the caller ID. I show the screen to Adrian. "I need to take this. He called once before and he's still my boss when this is over. Maybe. I don't know. He's my boss."

I answer the call, "Hi Ed," as Adrian pushes to his feet, grabbing the coffee pot to refill our cups.

"Do you have a slug of whiskey handy?" Ed asks. "Because you're going to need one."

"Oh God," I say, glancing at Adrian as he fills my cup with cream and arches a brow, as I add, "That doesn't sound good."

"It's not," Ed says. "I was served papers today in the Austin office. I had one of the staff open the envelope and fax me the contents of the documents. Your father's firm is suing our office for fraudulent activity on all of Ian Shelton's cases. In other words, any charges filed by Ian will be in question."

"Oh my God," I say and I can feel the blood drain from my cheeks, and at this point, Adrian is sitting next to me, watching me, concern in his face. And the concern is appropriate. We all need to be concerned right now because Ian was the ADA who was in charge of the Waters case before he left and I took over. "Tell me the lawsuit has no merit," I say. "Please tell me it has no merit, Ed."

"I'm looking at the documents supplied with the filing," he says grimly. "It doesn't look good, Pri. I believe we're in trouble. If Waters' defense takes this to the judge—"

"You think he'll dismiss the case? I'm back to please say no."

"He won't have a choice," Ed argues. "I'm flying back to Texas to face this. I'm already on a plane."

I frown. "Did Walker approve you traveling?"

Adrian nods and holds up his phone, clearly being updated by text as I am by phone.

"What if this is a ploy to get you out in the open, Ed? To kill you?"

Adrian gives me a look that says he agrees.

Ed, however, blows off the worry. "Walker is escorting me," he assures me, "but I can't stress enough that my actions are necessary. As I said, I saw the documents. This is the real deal. And for the record, it sucks that your father is behind it. This is the end of me. There's no question about it."

I swallow hard, hating that my father did this. Hating that I can't even call it wrong. I mean, his job is to protect his clients. If the documents are legit, then Ian is the one who did everyone dirty. "I don't know what to say right now," I murmur.

"What is there to say?" Ed asks. "Nothing. We're fucked. I've got to go, but don't be surprised if you hear from the judge. Call me if you talk to him before I do."

"Should we call him and give him a heads up?"

"I left him a message," he replies. "I'll let you know when I know more." He disconnects.

Shellshocked, I let the phone fall from my ear.

"I think you're about to get your wish," I say. "I think Waters is about to go free. I don't know what you know from Blake. Maybe all of it."

"Tell me anyway," Adrian urges.

"The attorney that charged him apparently did some dirty things on his cases. Most of them are in jeopardy of being dismissed. Including Waters."

"And your father filed the lawsuit," he supplies.

"He did, but I can't call that dirty, Adrian. He's protecting his clients. Of course, he's clearly doing it for Waters' benefit. I get that. Believe me, I get that in a brutal way." My cellphone buzzes with a text message and I glance down to find a file drop from Ed with a message that reads: *The documents. It's a shitshow that gets worse every time I look.*

I grab my computer where it sits on the kitchen island and shove my plate aside. "Ed sent me a copy of the legal filing."

"I'm going to call Blake while you look at it," Adrian says, already punching in the auto-dial on his phone.

I download the documents Ed sent me and he's right. It doesn't look good. And my father only filed on behalf of his own clients. More filings will follow. "Blake says Ed is expectedly frazzled," Adrian says. "He doesn't think he knew this was going to happen in advance."

"I'm sure he didn't," I say. "He likes his title and he's going to lose his job over this."

"Just keep in mind that Waters would bite the hand off his own kid if it meant survival. This doesn't mean Ed's not dirty. He may have just been burned or paid well enough to choose money and life over death."

My cellphone rings again and my stomach falls at the number on caller ID. "It's Judge Nichols. This can't be good." I draw a breath and answer the line. "Judge Nichols. Good morning."

"Do you know what's going on?" he asks, cutting right to the chase.

"I do," I say. "Unfortunately."

"Between you and I, I do not want to make the call this is forcing me to make. But Waters' defense has petitioned to have his case dropped. I'm by the book. I do things right and I don't always like what that means."

A boulder might as well have been slammed on my shoulders for the weight of his words. "You're dropping the charges?"

"Give me a reason not to," he says.

"I have witnesses and evidence, judge. He's a killer. He's a monster. He is the devil. Why would we let witnesses die only to have the case dismissed? Why are we all in hiding, if we're just letting him walk away?"

"Can you prove he had those witnesses killed?"

"No, but—"

"There is no 'but.' You can or you can't."

"I can't."

"Then re-arrest him and charge him again tomorrow after he gets out of jail. *If* you can get the District Attorney to approve it with this kind of mud on his face. Because right now, any conviction you get will be appealed. And you'll lose."

"Then you're dropping the charges? That's it?"

"Send me anything you want me to consider before I render my decision within the hour. I'll let you know my final ruling by morning." He disconnects.

Chapter Forty

PRI

The minute the judge hangs up on me, I call Ed. He picks up on the first ring. "The judge is going to let him out," I say. "We have to re-arrest him right after release. It's a ridiculous process. We'll let him walk out of the facility and just arrest him again. I'll get the paperwork together and—"

"No," he says. "We're not reliving this hell until we deal with this scandal. I'm not sure I'll even be here to make the call. A new District Attorney will likely make this call."

"Ed—"

"No," he snaps. "I just talked to the mayor, Pri. We have bodies stacking up and now, scandal. We're done. It's done." He disconnects.

I close my hand over my phone and stand up, shoving it in my pocket. Adrian is right in front of me. "That didn't sound good."

"It's not," I say. "It's done. He's letting him out." I round the barstool and walk to the window, staring out at the city. The rain has stopped. And my case is over. I've failed to win against the devil.

Adrian is with me, immediately in front of me, leaning on a steel beam and pulling me to him. "It's done," I say again because I just can't get my head around the idea of it, the reality of it. "He's going free. The judge said I could submit documents, but why bother? They won't change anything. Waters will be out of jail by morning. And there's nothing I can do about it. I mean, we *could* re-arrest him, I have the evidence, outside anything my predecessor did, to file charges, but Ed isn't going to let that happen. You were right. Waters' is unbeatable."

"I didn't say he was unbeatable," he reminds me. "I said there was only one way to beat him."

"You're going to kill him, and then go to jail." My hands go to his hands where they rest on my hips as if holding onto him somehow keeps him right here with me. "You'll go to jail, Adrian."

"I won't go to jail, Pri," he promises me. "That's not how this plays out."

My phone rings in my pocket, and reluctantly, oh so reluctantly, I retrieve it and glance down at the caller ID to find Logan calling. "Logan," I say.

"Ignore him," Adrian orders, hand catching my hip again. "You don't ever have to talk to him again."

"I have a bad feeling about the timing of the call," I say immediately. "I need to talk to him." I don't wait for his approval. I can't take any more surprises. I answer the call. "Logan, what the hell did you mean you've been protecting me? What don't I know?"

"I think you know now," he says dryly, arrogance in his tone.

"What does that mean?"

"It means I did nothing without the direction of your father. You wanted him to be your hero. I was your hero. I kept you from finding out just how dirty he is. He ended your case against Waters. He did. Your own father."

"He did it legally."

"Right. Legally." He snorts. "He always finds that sweet spot and keeps the dirt under the rug. And yes, I'm fine. Thanks for asking. You hit a fleshy area that will heal up nicely." His tone deepens. "The charges against Adrian have been dropped. Tell him it's a gift from a friend." He hangs up and I go cold.

Adrian catches my hand holding the phone. "What just happened?"

"The charges against you were dropped. He said it was a gift from a friend. He means Waters, of course."

"Yes," he says tightly. "He means Waters."

"Why would Waters do that?"

"It's an invitation to come and see him."

"I see," I say tightly. "I assume you plan to accept." It's not a question.

"Whatever I do will be on my terms, not his. So, this is the plan. We lay low and give Blake time to flush out all of the dirty players. He'll find out exactly where your father stands in all of this. Where Josh stands. Where Ed stands."

"And we do what?"

"We're still on a hitlist, Pri. We leave the country. We spend a month seeing Europe, and then we come back just in time for my brother's New Year's Eve event in Dallas. I'll tell him about Alex. And you'll be there with me. I need you there with me."

He needs me with him. My heart melts with that confession and I wrap my arms around him. "I can't leave until I know for sure Waters is released. But yes. Yes to everything. And I need to be there with you. I want to be there with you."

He strokes my hair. "I'll make the arrangements. Maybe when we get back, you'll know you want to spend the rest of your life with me."

"You think I need this trip to know that?"

"I'll ask properly when this is over, Pri. And you can tell me how you feel then. Deal?"

"Deal," I say and I'm in the moment with Adrian, and the month ahead that I know will be a fantasy. Because I don't know why Adrian is walking away from Waters right now, but I know it's part of a bigger plan. He's going after Waters and he won't stop until one of the two of them is dead.

Chapter Forty-One

PRI

I don't send anything over to the judge to consider before releasing Waters. There's just no point. He's made his decision. He will free the devil. The end. It's happening. I also don't talk to Ed again that day. Again, what's the point? Lucifer apparently has Grace with him, taking her to lunch and comforting her, which I fear is only going to make her crush all over him, but it's better than her crushing all over Josh. I believe that the love affair she'd had with him has expired.

Instead, Adrian shows me around the apartment, which includes a gym, two spare bedrooms, the library I'd seen earlier, and a weapons room with a padded firing range. I eagerly goggle up and spend an hour shooting, eager for Adrian's suggestions to improve my skills. But I can tell he's impressed and relieved I can handle my weapon.

Blake arrives about two o'clock with his wife Kara, who is a pretty brunette and an ex-FBI agent. The four of us sit around the kitchen island, steaming coffee in our cups.

"Obviously," I say, "my father is involved with Waters. I just want to know if he's trapped in the situation or if he's there willingly. Is there any way to know that?"

Adrian squeezes my leg beneath the table, telling me he understands, that he supports me, and I know he does. God, how I know after the story he told me last night. I cover his hand with mine, as Blake promises, "I'll find out. The question is, what do you want to do about either case?"

"I don't know," I say. "But knowledge is power. Once I know, I'll figure it out."

"Fair enough," he says. "I'll be in touch." He eyes Adrian. "I have a plane on standby for you for tomorrow."

Kara hands me a card. "This is Chrissy. She's a personal shopper. I called her and told her you might need her to grab you some things today."

"Oh perfect," I say. "Yes. I do."

"One more thing before we go, Pri," Blake says, sliding a folder in front of me. "That's a job offer. We have clients that need legal consultations in a discreet manner. You'd be paid well for your services."

"But I thought if I practiced law, Waters would find me," I say.

"He will," Blake confirms, "but you'll be off the books and using an alias for the consults."

"Don't you have people for this already?" I ask. "I don't want to be an obligation hire."

"We have a few attorneys we trust. Very few. We need more. I believe I can trust you. Think about it. No pressure. And you can work remotely, anywhere in the world." He stands and Kara joins him.

"Looking forward to getting to know you, Pri," Kara says, and then they're headed for the door.

Adrian shifts on his stool and we turn to face each other, legs pressed together intimately, his hand on my knee. "What do you think?"

"Do you need to walk them out?"

"They know their way around. What do you think?"

"About which part?"

"All of it."

I could tell him I was standing on a bridge over hell when I met him, and that it was about to break in half. I could tell him that he and his "family" kept me from falling in, but he'd tell me he put me front and center. And I'm not sure that's an argument I can win, even if I want to win it with all my heart. So instead, I say, "Where are we going in Europe?"

"Where do you want to go?"

"Everywhere with you," I say.

He smiles, this devastating handsome smile, with no hint of apprehension, and says, "Anywhere you want to go."

The afternoon and evening with Adrian are remarkably wonderful, considering all that is going on in our lives. The commitment we've made to each other has created this warm, intimate, deepening connection. Since we've both been to Rome and Venice, and both cities are a bit too high profile for us right now, we decide to start our trip in Italy exploring the small, wonderful beachfront communities, with one exception: a castle in Rome owned by a powerful friend of Adrian's, that he assures me is safe. From there, we'll go to France and Germany, where we'll stay at the home of another friend: the famous violinist Kace August, who Adrian ran a protection detail for last year.

Hours later, after I've placed and received a large order from the personal shopper, we're in the bedroom in front of the window, watching it rain yet again, enjoying the wine we'd abandoned last night when I say, "I'm going to resign with the DA's office."

"You sure you want to do that?"

"We both know it's necessary," I say, "and I feel remarkably at peace with it. I wanted to make a difference. I didn't. Maybe I can with Walker Security."

"Then you're going to take the job?"

"Yes," I say. "I do believe I will. Are you going to stay with Walker?"

"I do believe I owe them my loyalty."

"You do," I agree, and I open my mouth to tell him it will take getting used to, loving someone who is always in danger, but I bite back the silly words. Waters lives. Waters will be free. Waters will always be at our backs. So instead, I say, "Where will we live safely?"

He sips his wine and sets it down. "What about right here?"

I set my wine down and scoot closer to him. His arm wraps around my shoulders and my head settles on his chest. "I like it here," I say, but I don't ask how that would be possible.

We both know how it would be possible.

Us or him. Is that really what our life has come down to?

My cellphone rings and I glance at the number to find Judge Nichols calling. I answer the line with, "Judge."

"Sorry for the late call, but I thought you had the right to know. I'm dismissing the charges."

"When does he get out?"

"Ten tomorrow morning. I wish I had better news."

"Me, too," I say and I disconnect, glancing at Adrian. "Tomorrow at ten in the morning. I'm sure it will be televised."

"Then we'll watch from the plane," he says, retrieving his phone and making the arrangements.

The next day, Adrian and I are on a private jet owned by Walker Security by nine AM. Savage and his wife Candace are with us as well. Candace is an architect, it turns out, and funny, sweet, and gorgeous. Her dark hair is silk. Her green eyes are bright. The two of us end up sitting at a small booth while Adrian and Savage chat with Blake, who has just boarded the plane.

She tells me all about Savage leaving her to "save" her.

"But he came back," I say, stating the obvious.

"He did," she says, "but it isn't always easy being in love with a man who has enemies. His enemies are my enemies, but I don't care. He's the love of my life. We belong together."

I think of the assassin named Michael. I wonder who he is and how he knows Savage.

And I think of Adrian's parents. Someone killed them. Someone who wanted his father out of the way. Adrian has enemies, too. He will always have enemies.

"Savage is a complicated man," Candace adds. "His life is complicated, but when we're together, it's not complicated at all. It's just us."

She just summarized every moment I've ever shared with Adrian.

A few minutes later, the lot of us—me, Adrian, Savage, Candace, Blake, and even Kara, are sitting in a large lounge area with the news coverage on, watching the anticipation of the King Devil's release. Suddenly, he's on the screen, smiling at the cameras.

"Would you like to give a statement?" one reporter shouts and many other shouts follow.

Waters waves them off, seemingly uninterested in the attention. The police push back the press and Waters walks toward a fancy sports car at the prison gates and clicks the locks. He climbs inside the vehicle.

"Piece of shit," Savage murmurs, while Adrian says nothing.

He just watches.

Waters cranks the engine and drives away, pulling off onto the highway, and disappearing in the distance. "And so it's done," I say, but then there is chaos on the news screen, people running everywhere, and a camera pans to smoke lifting off the highway just over the hill.

The news anchor then says, "It appears that there has been an explosion. I repeat, it appears there has been an explosion." He listens in his earpiece and then says, "I've confirmed that Nick Waters' vehicle has blown up with him inside of it. He is presumed dead."

"I didn't do it," Savage says. "In case anyone's wondering. I'm a more hands-on and in-your-face kind of killer."

All of us are now looking at Adrian. "It wasn't me," he says. "I didn't kill him or have him killed. But I would have. Someone beat me to the punch."

"I can't believe this is happening," I say. "I mean—I can't believe it's *really happening*. Waters is dead and I feel like a bad person for saying this, but I'm relieved. It's over for us."

Adrian's jaw clenches. "No. It's not over. Deleon is still alive."

Chapter Forty-Two

PRI

Adrian and I spend the holidays in Europe. Thanksgiving is a feast by the water in an amazing spot off of the Italian Riviera. Christmas is in Rome, in the castle Adrian's friend owns, and it's magnificent. His friend, or friends rather, Kayden and Ella Wilkens, are wonderful, as is their housekeeper and live-in mom of sorts, Marbella, who fills our bellies with wonderful food. And their tree is gorgeous and so big, that it fills the impressively large front foyer of the castle.

On Christmas morning, I wake to Adrian telling me a bad joke before we ever get out of bed. "What do you call a kid who doesn't believe in Santa?"

"Okay, I'll bite. What do you call a kid who doesn't believe in Santa?"

"A rebel without a Claus."

I laugh and a few minutes later, we are enjoying coffee and croissants thanks to Marabella, and the two of us have cozied up in front of the fireplace in our room, me in a fuzzy warm robe, and him in nothing but his pajama bottoms, as we prepare to exchange gifts. Thankfully when I'd gone shopping with Ella a few days earlier, I'd found something special. I offer Adrian the small silver-wrapped box. "You first," I insist.

He doesn't argue and I can see the curiosity in his eyes, but also something quite thoughtful. "The last gift I got for Christmas was from my parents the year before they died."

Considering all I know of the friends around him, this surprises me. "Not even from your friends at Walker?"

"I was on a mission overseas last year during Christmas."

And hating himself for killing Alex, I think. I decide to bring him back to a more sentimental memory, praying it's not painful. "Tell me about the gift, the last one your parents got you."

Fortunately, the question immediately stirs his laughter. "Aside from socks? My mother always gave me socks. She said I never bought the basics for myself. Every year no matter how old I got, she gave me socks."

I laugh now, too. "Socks are very necessary."

"Yes. And they—Mom and Dad—they gave me an AC/DC album. A sentimental thing from when I was a kid. I used to crank the music up and piss everyone off."

"Sounds like a special gift," I say, my chest pinching slightly at the dart of pain I see in his eyes.

"It was," he says solemnly. There is joy and pain in this memory, that is clear. "I framed it," he adds, that statement telling me just how fond this memory is he's shared, how important it is to him. "I'll show it to you when we get home," he promises and then shifts the topic to me. "What about you? What are your Christmases normally like?"

"Awkward and filled with expensive gifts that had no emotional value at all. Obligation gifts." I wave off what is easily dismissed, and painfully remember and focus on the here and now, the good times. "Open the gift," I urge. "I'm really excited to give you your present."

He hesitates just a moment as if he wants to ask me questions about my past, but then he caves to my request. His lips curve and he does my bidding. He opens the box, removing the small leather box inside. He opens it and glances down at the hand-crafted watch with a wooden finish. "Made by a famous craftsman here in Italy."

"I love it," he says. "It's interesting in a good way."

"Turn it over," I say, my heart fluttering with a hint of nerves that really have no place in this moment, except I am putting my heart on the line here a bit. Something he'll know soon. "It's the engraving on the back I want you to see," I add.

His eyes warm and he flips the watch, his eyes landing on the words etched in the wood, reading them out loud, "Every moment with you makes me want a lifetime." His eyes immediately meet mine and then he's pulling me close, kissing me, and it is not *just* a kiss. It's passion and love. And it's friendship. Because that is what we have become. Best friends and lovers.

"I love it," he says softly. "And you. I love you, Pri."

"And I love you, Adrian Mack."

He gently strokes my hair behind my ear, his fingers teasing my skin, goosebumps lifting in their wake. His eyes are warm, a sea of invitation that says, stay with me, be with me. This is where you belong.

"Your turn," He says softly before he hands me a small flat box wrapped in red paper. I quickly tear away the wrapping, nervous all over again, over an intimate moment, that feels as if it's about to tell me a story, that I'm eager to read. Inside the paper I find a beautiful wooden box with an intricate cross etched in the center. I open the lid to discover a necklace—a silver and diamond infinity cross. "Infinity," I say softly, and look at him, aware of the meaning of this gift—it's him telling me he wants us to be forever and my heart swells with that message. "It's beautiful," I say, emotion rasping in the depths of my reply.

"And so are you," he says, reaching for the box. "I'll help you put it on."

He eases behind me, and I swear I'm so hyperaware of Adrian right now, my nipples pucker with the anticipation of his touch that isn't even sexual.

"Hold up your hair," he says, and then he's sliding the necklace around me, his touch light, but I feel it intensely. Once the cross falls between my breasts, he kisses my neck, and whispers, "Infinity and more, baby."

Chapter Forty-Three

PRI

We land in New York and Savage, Lucifer, and Adam all join us for the flight to Texas and Rafael's concert. A group event planned the week before when Adrian had called his brother on speakerphone, introduced me, and made the arrangements. The two brothers' excitement to see each other again had been palpable. Once we're in flight, Lucifer joins Adrian and me in the lounge to update us on the Walker investigation, into, well, just about everyone I know.

"Ed is dirty," he says, "and so is Josh. We've handed over the data we've collected to the Feds. They'll be dealt with."

I don't ask for details. I'm exhausted by details right now but also worried about my friend. "And Grace?" I ask. "Is she safe? And yes, I mean, from everyone, including you."

Lucifer gives a low chuckle. "I'm the one who needs protection from Grace. She's an animal."

My eyes go wide and he holds up his hands. "I'm joking. We're friends. That's all. She's all good and plenty safe. You should call her. She'd love to hear from you."

"I will," I say and if he senses what is coming, Adrian wraps his arm around me and asks the next question for me. "And Pri's parents?"

"They do shady shit over there at your father's firm, Pri," he replies, "but for the most part, your father finds a way to keep it all legal. Barely, but legal."

My brows knit. "But what about the claim that he was laundering money for Waters?"

"I can't find proof," Lucifer replies. "Do I think it happened? Yes. Do I think he was blackmailed? Yes. Do I think they have someone really fucking good covering their trails over there? Yes. I'll keep digging if you really want me to. Just keep in mind that if I dig, I'll eventually find the truth."

The truth, I repeat in my head. Do I really want the truth? I've talked to my mother once since Waters was killed. She asked me to coffee. She had no idea I wasn't in the country. She'd said she wanted to "mend fences," whatever that means. My father had called a week later, right after I'd faxed my formal resignation to Ed. I hadn't answered the call. He'd left a voicemail: *You made a good decision leaving the DA's office. Come home.*

Come home doesn't mean to Texas. He meant back to work for his firm, where I would be expected to be his compliant little daughter.

I blink Lucifer back into view. "Just leave it alone," I say and I offer no other explanation. I'm not sure what to do about my family and it's something I need to think about and talk to Adrian about when we're alone.

"Message received," Lucifer says, "but one last big thing. Your father fired Logan and Logan abruptly left the state."

"Good," I say, and in my mind, I can't help but hope that Logan is the one who got my father involved in all of this and my father saw the light. But that's a daughter's hero complex. And my father is no hero.

About the time, I'm about to drag Adrian to a more private location to talk Savage sits down, a beer in hand. "A man walks into a bar," he says, pointing at Adrian. "Give it to me, baby. One of those horrible jokes of yours."

I laugh, my mood lighter already. "He told me a hundred bad jokes in Italy alone," I say, eyeing him. "Come on. A man walks into a bar. Go."

Adrian rubs his hands together. "A man walks into a bar owned by Eminem. He tells the bartender, 'Give me two shots of—' The bartender cuts him off saying, 'You only get one shot.'"

We all groan at the reference to Eminem's most popular song, "Lose Yourself" and already Adrian launches into another joke. "A man walks into a bar—"

I touch the necklace he gave me and warmth fills me. This is my family. He is my family. And I will never get tired of his jokes.

Chapter Forty-Four

PRI

We don't talk about Deleon before we land in Texas, but I know there's a reason, outside of friendship, that we're surrounded by the Walker family. And apparently so is Rafael, I discover. His entire security team is part of Walker Security. In that way, I know Adrian has shown him his love. He's not been with him, and yet, he has been looking after him.

We land in Texas and head straight for the concert. With backstage passes, Adrian and I are quickly united with his brother. The two of them come together with an embrace, and they hold that pose for a solid minute. "Damn, I missed you, brother," Adrian murmurs.

"Me, too, man," Rafael says, looking at Adrian. "I missed the hell out of you."

They look so alike, and they share a similar energy. I can't help but wonder if Alex favored them. I decide he couldn't have. There's no way he did the things Adrian described and was anything like these two brothers.

Adrian pulls me forward and introduces me properly to Rafael despite us having met by phone last week. "Hello, Pri," Rafael greets. "Good to meet you. I guess he hasn't told you his bad jokes yet since you've stuck around."

I laugh. "You have no idea how many bad jokes I've heard."

Someone calls out Rafael's name and speaks to him in Spanish. "Gotta run now," he says, shaking my hand. "We'll talk after the show."

He hugs Adrian again. "You finally made my show."

"And I'm proud as a motherfucker, man."

Rafael's expression lights. He likes this compliment from his brother. He's a superstar and the world loves him, but it's family he needs. *They* need each other.

ADRIAN

The concert is amazing.

My little brother on that stage, in fancy outfits, owning his stardom, deserving it. He's a better man than Alex or I ever were. Humble. Kind. Generous. And I don't think about anything outside of the moment. Pri sings and dances, and so do we all. Savage is an absolute savage. The man is a huge fan of my brother's. Who'd have believed it? When it's all over, my brother doesn't even consider some big party, not even on New Year's Eve. He's never been the party guy and stardom hasn't changed that, apparently. Raf is back in his favorite jeans, boots, and a T-shirt in no time. And since he needs out of the limelight, with hordes of fans looking for him, me, Pri, and our team, follow his bus to a small town about an hour out of the city, and stop at a diner.

For a good hour, me, Pri, and Rafael sit at a table, talking and eating, while Savage and Lucifer hit the bar next door. Adam and Jacob, who have become Raf's personal guard until the Deleon threat passes, hang out in the diner with us, but at their own table. Eventually, we all go next door, and Raf and I end up at a pool table. "Like old times," he says. "A perfect way to start a new year."

"Amen to that, brother," I say, tilting back my beer, aware of Pri nearby.

She's at a table with Savage and Lucifer, laughing, and I know intentionally giving me space with Raf. I love that woman. I love the hell out of her like I didn't know I could love. And for a while I just let me and Raf be brothers, and it's good, so good I'm not sure I want to ruin it by talking about Alex.

We eventually head outside for some air, sitting on a concrete wall that frames the bar, and staring up at the clear night sky. "I miss you, man," Raf says, glancing over at me. "I miss Mom and Dad. Sometimes I even miss Alex, but the Alex who pretended to be like us, you know?" He glances over at me. "He died a hero, right? That's how he left this world."

"Do you want him to be a hero, Raf, or do you want to know the truth? Your choice."

"The truth. I want nothing but the truth between you and me, Adrian. We're all we got left."

I look skyward, drawing in a breath. "You know we both went under in the Devil's biker gang. What you don't know is that we both thought they were connected to Mom and Dad's deaths."

"Were they? Are they?"

"We never proved it. I don't know. We may never know. But Alex—I knew that life was trouble for him and I was right. It was like a drug. The women. The drugs. The violence."

"He had it in him," Raf says. "He always did. It never made sense. He wasn't like us."

"No, he wasn't. I killed him, Raf. He was attacking a woman. I tried to stop him. He killed her and drew on me. It was me or him. I know that, but it haunts me. You have no fucking idea."

"Is this where I'm supposed to freak the fuck out and ask you how you dared do such a thing?" he asks. "Because that's not happening. I know who he was. I saw him. More than you, I think. He didn't hide shit from me because I was so young. I think he didn't see me as a threat. The right man lived, Adrian. The right man lived."

Relief washes over me, but the guilt is still there in my gut, eating me alive. "I know, and yet, I don't know."

"You need to know. And I can see you love Pri. It's in your eyes. Let her help. I like her. Marry her. I like that idea. Do you like that idea?"

"I'm fucking in love with that idea," I say. "But Deleon is still out there. I need to clean this up before I marry her."

At that moment, Pri and Savage exit the bar. "What's up?" Savage wails. "What's up?!"

"Your booze intake," I say dryly. "Or you wouldn't be so loud."

"I'm always loud," he says. "Well, unless I'm about to kill someone. *Then* I walk like a little bitty church mouse." He uses his fingers to show the walking. "Little bitty and oh so quiet." He's whispering. And now he's laughing. "I need to call my baby. I should have brought her. All is well here. She loves Rafael." He points at Raf. "Not like me, but she loves you, man."

Rafael is laughing while Pri gives us an apologetic look. "Sorry, guys," she says. "The bathroom is stopped up. I need to go to the restaurant and use that one, but turns out, that even drunk, Savage is protective. He won't let me go alone."

"You can use the one on the bus," Raf says. "I'll walk you. I want to grab a photo to show Adrian." He snags keys from his pocket and motions Pri forward.

She kisses me. "Okay?"

"Of course, baby. Raf's bus is fancy as fuck."

"I mean you," she says softly. "Are *you* okay?"

She's worried about me. I don't have to let that sink in. I drink that shit up. I need it. I need the hell out of this woman "Never better," I promise. "I'll tell you everything later."

She smiles a tiny smile meant only for me and then turns away, motioning to my brother. Her and Raf start walking toward the bus. I watch them, and it's a magic moment, something shifting inside me, some of the darkness fading away. *Family*. This is my family.

PRI

I'm aware of Jacob following me and Raf toward the bus, and the need for this kind of close supervision is a reminder that Deleon is out there. Well, of course, I am walking with a superstar, who likely needs round-the-clock protection anyway. That's a comforting thought. There is more to our lives than Waters.

"Tonight was fun," I say, trying to tune out everything but the brother of the man I love. "Thank you for putting us in the front row. Funny story. Adrian was undercover when we met." I smile. "He told me his name was Rafael."

He laughs. "Please tell me he didn't tell you he was me."

"No," I say. "But the fact that he used your name as an alias tells me you were always on his mind."

"As he was mine," he says, giving me a warm smile. "Thank you for that. And thank you for being here with him. He needs you. That's clear." He stops walking and turns to face me. "He told me about Alex's final moments."

"And?"

"And you already knew," he observes.

"I did," I confirm.

"He trusts you," he concludes.

"I hope so. I really do."

"He does," he assures me. "I need him to be okay, Pri. Are you going to stay around and make sure he's okay?"

"I am. I absolutely am. I love him."

"Good," he says and motions me forward. "Good. You'll think these photos are fun, I bet."

We start walking again and I have no idea why, but this strong sense of unease comes over me.

We reach the bus and Rafael is about to click the locks. I cover his hand. "Don't. Something feels wrong. Let's go back. Let's go back now." He gives me one look, seemingly weighing my words and expression, and must see the terror ripping through my gut. He doesn't question me.

In unison, we turn and start running. Jacob is instantly charging toward us, trying to find the danger. In an instant, he's all but on top of us, and he's drawn his weapon, letting us pass him, holding the ground.

And that's when the explosion happens.

Chapter Forty-Five

ADRIAN

When Pri and Raf start running, I start running.

Everything is in slow motion. I don't know what is happening, but I know it's bad.

I run hard and fast, the burn in my legs, launching me forward. I'm almost to Pri and Raf when the explosion happens but almost isn't good enough. I watch my brother throw himself on top of Pri. The impact shakes the ground and forces me down, huddled against the ground, metal flying everywhere. I'm up the minute I can get up, grabbing my brother, who is thank fuck, pushing to his feet. "I'm fine. I'm okay," he pants out. "Pri. Check Pri."

He's barely spoken the words, and I'm already on the ground, pulling Pri into my arms. "Pri. Baby."

"I'm okay," she says, grabbing my arm and coughing. "I'm okay." She swallows hard. "I swallowed soot," she whispers, rubbing her throat. "I'm good now."

I cup her face. "Are you sure you're okay? Tell me you're sure."

"I am," she promises, her hands on my hands. "Rafael. Rafael. And Jacob."

"I'm clear," Jacob says from somewhere nearby. "I'm good."

I ease Pri to her feet, checking her, wiping away more of the soot that choked her, moments before. "God, woman, you scared me. You scared the fuck out of me." I fold her close. "You don't get to die on me." I cup her head. "Ever. Ever." I lean back to look at her. "Do you understand?"

Savage appears beside us, grabbing both of our arms. "Dr. Savage here. Let me take a look at both of you. Sit. That means girls and boys take a seat."

Adam shoves a chair under Pri that I assume he got from the bar and she sits before he talks with Jacob a few steps away. Savage cuffs Pri to check her blood pressure and I kneel beside her. "What made you run?" I ask. "How did you know what was coming?"

Savage agrees. "Exactly my question."

"It was just a gut instinct," Pri replies. "I can't explain it. Suddenly, I was suffocating in a bad feeling."

"Holy hell," Raf says, joining us, obviously overhearing. "Thank God for your bad feelings, Pri."

I push to my feet and give the big, soot-covered bastard a hug. "Don't die asshole."

"She saved my life, man," he says, when we break away, he adds. "She saved us both. We were lucky. Who did this?"

"Waters," I say. "Waters did this."

Adam, clearly eavesdropping, joins our circle, and says, "Waters is dead, Adrian."

"No, he's not" I assure him. "He's not dead. I promise you he got out of that car before it exploded. There's a reason why it happened off-camera. I don't know how he did it, but he did it. And he just fucking loves symbolism. His car blew up. The bus blew up. That's him telling me this was him." I look at Raf.

"Walker is going to get you to safety. Go with them. Stay with them until I get back." I turn to Adam. "Get him and Pri someplace safe."

"Where are you going, Adrian? What are you going to do?"

"He expects me to come. I'm not going to let him down." I try to turn away.

Raf catches my arm. "Adrian—"

"You and Pri will never be safe until I do this. I'm doing this." I pull away from him before he demands I define "this" and walk to Pri.

"She's good," Savage says, helping Pri to her feet. "She's a dirty, dirty girl with no restrictions. She's all yours, man."

Pri shoots him an "are you serious" look as Jacob joins us. "I searched the area," Jacob announces. "Nothing. I found nothing. And I saw nothing. Pri is the one who reacted. What did you see?"

Pri stands and huddles close to me, while talking to the group, repeating what I've already heard. "Nothing. It was just this crazy gut feeling."

I turn her to face me, hands on her shoulders. "I need you to let Adam and Jacob get you to safety. I'll come for you soon."

"Why would I go with them? Where are you going?"

"I have to end this once and for all, Pri. I know you know I do."

"You mean kill Deleon," she assumes. "Adrian—"

"Waters. This was Waters, Pri. This was him. He's not dead. Not yet."

"No," she says. "He died."

"He faked his death. I'll bet my life on it."

Her fingers curl around my shirt. "No, you will not. Because you made me love you and now you do not get to die." Her voice rasps with demand. "Do you hear me?"

I fold her close and cup her face. "I love you."

"You can't—"

Emergency crews erupt onto the scene around us. I ignore them and kiss her, I kiss the hell out of her right there in front of everyone. And when I'm done, I don't give her time to argue. I hand her off to Jacob. "Keep her safe. Get her back to New York."

She lunges for me and Adam is there, catching her from behind. I turn away from her and start walking while she screams after me. Leaving her guts me, but losing her because I let Waters and Deleon live is not an option.

Savage is by my side in an instant, falling into step with me.

I flick him a look. "Where the hell do you think you're going, Savage?"

"With you, my perfect revenge-seeking motherfucker. And if you don't like it, we can fight, but I'd win and that would hurt your confidence, so let's not."

I don't answer. He wouldn't win. Not right now. I'm too focused. I'm too ready to do what I should have done a long time ago. Kill the devil.

Chapter Forty-Six

ADRIAN

The Devils' clubhouse is four hours from the location where I left Pri and Raf. Savage and I take one of the Walker vehicles and drive into Dallas. Once we're there, we meet up with the local Walker team, who loads us up with firearms and allows us to shower off the soot and change clothes. Shortly after that meet-up, Blake calls me for the fifth time. I decline the call. He calls Savage.

"Bossman is calling," Savage says. "I take it we're ignoring him?"

"I am," I say, pulling us into a Ducati dealership. A bike riding into a biker club, unnoticed, is a whole lot easier than an SUV. I open the door. Savage declines the call and does the same.

An hour later, we've paid the dealership to store our vehicle and we ride into a cheap hotel on our Ducatis. Waters is a Harley guy. He hates Ducati and that's just all the more reason I should ride one to kill him. Every time I think of Pri on the ground, under my brother, while that bus exploded over the top of them, I want blood.

I kick back on the bed, aware that I need rest to face what is before me. Savage walks to the liquor store next door, grabs booze and burgers from some diner nearby. I down the burger and a few shots.

Savage doesn't speak. He doesn't tell his stupid stories. Death is serious business. And death is in the air.

I kick back on the bed, and my cellphone rings with Pri's number on the caller ID. I decline the call. I can't talk to her right now. I need to stay focused and strong to save her life. And that's what I'm doing. I'm saving her life. I'm making a path for our future.

I shut my eyes, and I dream, not of that future.

But of Waters. I dream of every monstrous thing he did when I was with him. And when I wake up, it's fuel.

It's late afternoon on New Year's Day when Savage and I hit the road, both in jeans, boots, and jackets to stave off the sun and bugs. It's a cooler day, but the wind is high, the roads busy with holiday travelers.

We arrive in Waco, Texas as the sun slides beneath the horizon. It's Saturday night, which means a party, regardless of the aftermath of New Year's Eve. The closer I get to the ranch the Devils call home, the angrier I become, and yet, the more focused.

I halt right outside the property line, and Savage does the same. I rip off my helmet and latch it to the side of the bike, but I don't dismount. Again, Savage does the same.

"What's the plan?"

"Find a good view of the property. I'll be at the back of the clubhouse. If I die, kill Waters and Deleon. I'll make sure you know who they are."

"Better yet, let's do it together. We're like Thelma and Louise, road trip buddies."

"Thelma and Louise died, and they were women."

"Okay then, you picky-ass bitch," he grumbles. "Name another movie."

"I'm going in, Savage. And don't fucking kill them. They tried to kill my brother and my woman. These are *my kills.*"

His lips press together. "Don't die."

I rev my engine and set the Ducati in motion. A mile up the road, the clubhouse is in view but there's no guard on duty. Why would there be? *What fool walks into a snake's nest? The kind who doesn't know how to avoid falling in the pit,* I think, but I do.

Tonight is fight night, the club's version of the UFC.

I park the bike and I'm off, focused, calm. I walk around the clubhouse to the left, and then to the back. At least thirty guys, and a dozen women, huddle around the fight circle with hard rock, booze, sex, and drugs lighting up the night more than the fire. At the head of that circle, I'll find Waters, on a ridiculous throne, with Deleon by his side. I enter the mix as if I belong when I never belonged here, but not one of these fools even notices me. That is until I step into the circle. And that's when I find Waters, on his throne, alive and well. He has a redheaded woman named Bella on his lap. He's abused that woman for years of her life and today, I'll take her with me when I leave. I'll make sure she's free.

As for Waters, he looks good, muscled up, healthy, a few new tats brightening up his right arm. I know everything about him. I spent years studying him. Learning him. Wanting to kill him.

For a moment, no one notices me, and then suddenly Waters' eyes meet mine. He sets Bella aside and lifts a hand and shouts out a command of, "Silence!" The music cuts off. Everyone is silent.

"I was expecting you, Adrian," Waters says. "Nice of you not to disappoint."

"Bold of you," I counter, "to wait for me here when you're supposed to be dead."

"I wanted to be sure you found me," he says, his lips curved in amusement.

"Kind of you not to make me hunt you down and kill you. Instead, I can do it here."

Deleon stands. "You're the one who's going to die tonight."

The crowd starts chanting, "Fight, fight, fight."

I step deeper into the circle. "Bring it. Unless you're afraid, Deleon."

He snorts. "Afraid of you? Never."

"I seem to remember planting your face in the floor and tying you up the last time we met."

Deleon, always easily provoked, folds his shoulders forward, and steps into the circle. "Piece of shit FBI agent. I'll show you to hell."

The chants continue and Waters lifts a hand. "Silence!"

The chants stop. "Fight to the death, Adrian."

"If he dies, you fight me," I say. "You prove you deserve to be King."

His lips press together. "You'd like that."

"I'd love that," I assure him. "You wouldn't. Deal?"

The crowd is watching and when the King is challenged, he must answer. That's how the club works. "Deal," he says. "But if I live, and you die, I promise you, Rafael and Priscilla will not survive my wrath as they did last night."

Deleon lunges at me with a knife when the fight is supposed to be bare-handed. He was always a cheater. The crowd erupts.

And while I held back the last time I fought Deleon because Pri was watching, I'm not this time. In my mind's eye, I see that explosion behind her and I know how easily she could be dead right now. I dodge Deleon's lunge, come up behind him, knock the knife out of his hand, and shove him to the ground. By the time he scrambles around, face down to face up, I'm over the top of him. This fight shouldn't be this easy—he and I have always been well-matched, but tonight, *it is* that easy. I slam the knife into his heart. And then he's dead.

The crowd goes eerily silent.

Waters draws in a deep breath, his chin lifting slightly. He stands, a beast of a man, a killer, who unlike Deleon, will not die easily. He steps into the center of the circle and we stand toe-to-toe.

"You should never have betrayed me," he says softly, the devil in his voice and eyes.

"You should never have come after my brother and my woman."

"Then you admit she's your woman," he replies dryly. "Good. Now I know to fuck her before I kill her."

He's trying to provoke me into making the first move, but I don't make the first move. I wait. I wait until the crowd roars and Waters' ego says he must act. He throws a punch. I duck and backup. He charges me, and we begin what becomes a brutal back and forth. He's down. I'm down. He's down again and I see Pri's face in my mind, and that's all it takes. I'm choking the hell out of him, but someone hits me from behind.

My ears ring and the world spins. I fall off of Waters, and he's on top of me, hitting me. *Pri*, I whisper in my mind. *Pri*. I gouge his eye and he roars, falling off of me and I press him to his back, landing a

LISA RENEE JONES

knee in his groin. Someone hits me again from behind and I whirl on a guy named Ted, a wannabe Deleon.

I grab him from behind, and I choke him the fuck out, letting him drop to the ground. At this point, Waters is recovering, on his knees, about to get up. That's when Bella steps to the circle with a gun in her hand. She's shaking, tears streaming down her face.

"Bella," I say. "I will help you. You don't have to do this."

And then to my shock, she turns to Waters and shoots him. And then shoots him again. And again. She drops the gun and Waters lets out a gurgling laugh before he falls face-first into the dirt.

He's dead, not by my hand, but at the hand of a woman he's abused.

I wish it could have been me, not for the revenge, but to save Bella the aftermath. She killed him. That will haunt her forever, but Waters will never touch her, or anyone else, again.

Chapter Forty-Seven

PRI

After nearly three days have passed since Raf and I arrived at Adrian's apartment with no word from Adrian or Savage, we're both losing our minds. It getting late, the night sky promising yet another night will pass without Adrian coming home. Adam and Jacob, who are taking turns babysitting us, have tried to offer comfort, but to no avail. Raf and I just want Adrian home. Or at least to answer his phone.

At present, Adam is upstairs watching television while Raf and I play cards at the kitchen island.

"I'm fairly certain Adam's choice of televisions is his way of assuring us he doesn't have to hover because we're safe here," Raf says, as his cellphone buzzes on the counter. He eyes the caller ID and sighs. "And that would be my management calling for the fifth time in three hours. And the fifth time I haven't answered. They want to know when my tour starts again."

"Are you worried they're going to reach a limit?"

"I'm worried about Adrian," he says. "They can wait." He yawns. "Damn," he murmurs. "I'm shockingly tired."

"It's not shocking at all," I say. "Neither of us has rested. You should try to sleep. You do have a tour to get back to."

"I might go and try to lay down a bit, but not because of the tour. Screw the tour," he says, and I can tell he's really not worried about his management. He's a star. His bus blew up. His people have to know his safety is in play here.

Raf stands up, still fully dressed in jeans and a T-shirt, and I suspect he feels as I do—a need to be ready for anything. "Don't you think Walker has to know more than they're telling us?" he asks.

It's a conversation we've had over and over again, but I'm all in. "I do, but I was thinking about that. What if Adrian and Savage haven't found Waters? Maybe they dumped their phones and haven't called in?"

"Or something worse," he says. "And on that note, I'm going to grab a bottle of whiskey, of which my brother has plenty, and drink myself to sleep." He holds up a hand. "Not a normal habit, but I think I'll make an exception."

"Understood," I say. "Goodnight."

"Are you going to try to rest?" he asks, giving me a worried look.

"Soon," I promise.

He hesitates but heads up the stairs. I stand up, comfy in my leggings and a tank top that I will sleep in if I sleep at all. Because as I sense in Raf, I just need to be dressed and ready if anything happens. I'm not sure what "anything" means, but I just need to be ready. Antsy, nervous, needing Adrian to just call me, I grab my phone, walk to the window, and dial Blake. He doesn't answer. Of course, he doesn't answer. I try Lucifer. He doesn't answer. "Damn them," I whisper, and stare out at the city lights, that twinkle like a lighthouse calling Adrian home.

I settle onto the couch and pull a blanket to my neck. At some point, I lay down and doze off, but it's a light sleep. A hum wakes me and I jolt into a sitting position. Awareness overtakes me and I stand up to find Adrian exiting the elevator. Relief, joy, and more relief have me flying around the couch. He rushes toward me as well. He's in jeans and a T-shirt, his jawline shadowed, his thick dark hair in disarray, but he is so damn tall, dark, and perfect. And in a flash that isn't fast enough in my book, I'm in his arms.

He cups my head and kisses me and it's the best kiss of my life, filled with so much need and so much happiness.

"Oh my God," I whisper. "I thought you were dead. I was so scared. What happened? Is Waters—"

"Dead," he says. "And so is Deleon. And no, I'm not going to jail. I've been dealing with the Feds for the past twelve hours. It's over, Pri. Really over. And I'll tell you all about it later. Right now, I have something important to ask you." He goes down on his knee and presents me with a velvet box. He opens the lid and I gasp at the gorgeous halo-shaped diamond ring, with an infinity design on each side of the band.

"I bought this when I bought the necklace. I just wanted Waters behind us before I gave it to you. But I want you to know that's how long I've wanted to say this. Marry me, Pri. You are my best friend. You are my everything. Forever. Be my wife."

Tears well in my eyes. "You are my everything," I say. "Forever. Yes. I would very much like to be your wife."

He smiles and slides the ring on my finger and cheers and clapping explode from above. Adrian and I glance up to find Rafael and Adam as our audience. We both laugh and Adrian kisses me. *Family*, I think. We're a family. And it's a wonderful thing.

THE END

Thank you so much for joining me on Adrian and Pri's journey! I hope you loved every minute of it! Have you read Savage's series? The finale is out on April 27th! You have just enough time to binge-read!

GET BOOKS ONE, TWO AND THREE, AND PRE-ORDER BOOK FOUR HERE:

https://www.lisareneejones.com/savage-series.html

If you loved the other Walker Security men, check out the other series from that world: Tall, Dark, and Deadly and Walker Security!

Don't forget, if you want to be the first to know about upcoming books, giveaways, sales and any other exciting news I have to share please be sure you're signed up for my newsletter! As an added bonus everyone receives a free ebook when they sign-up!

http://lisareneejones.com/newsletter-sign-up/

The Brilliance Trilogy

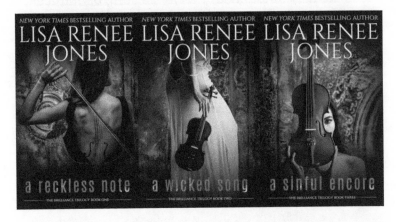

It all started with a note, just a simple note hand written by a woman I didn't know, never even met. But in that note is perhaps every answer to every question I've ever had in my life. And because of that note, I look for her, but find him. I'm drawn to his passion, his talent, a darkness in him that somehow becomes my light, my life. Kace August is rich, powerful, a rock star of violins, a man who is all tattoos, leather, good looks and talent. He has a wickedly sweet ability to play the violin, seducing audiences worldwide. Now, he's seducing me. I know he has secrets. I don't care. Because you see, I have secrets, too.

I'm not Aria Alard, as he believes. I'm Aria Stradivari, daughter to Alessandro Stradivari, a musician born from the same blood as the man who created the famous Stradivarius violin. I am as rare as the mere 650 instruments my ancestors created. Instruments worth millions. 650 masterpieces, the brilliance unmatched. 650 reasons to kill. 650 reasons to hide. One reason not to: him.

FIND OUT MORE ABOUT THE BRILLIANCE TRILOGY HERE:

https://www.lisareneejones.com/brilliance-trilogy.html

GET BOOK ONE, A RECKLESS NOTE, FREE EXCLUSIVELY HERE:

https://claims.prolificworks.com/free/sYEuj2pM

Excerpt from the Savage Series

> I NEED TO KISS HER AGAIN, JUST ONE MORE TIME BEFORE I DIE. AND I'M NOT SURE WHEN I DO, I'LL BE ABLE TO WALK AWAY.
>
> SAVAGE HUNGER
> NEW YORK TIMES BESTSELLING AUTHOR
> LISA RENEE JONES

He's here.

Rick is standing right in front of me, bigger than life, and so damn him, in that him kind of way that I couldn't explain if I tried. He steps closer and I drop my bag on the counter. He will hurt me again, I remind myself, but like that first night, I don't seem to care.

I step toward him, but he's already there, already here, right here with me. I can't even believe it's true. He folds me close, his big, hard body absorbing mine. His fingers tangle in my hair, his lips slanting over my lips. And then he's kissing me, kissing me with the intensity of a man who can't breathe without me. And I can't breathe without him. I haven't drawn a real breath since he sent me that letter.

My arms slide under his tuxedo jacket, wrapping his body, muscles flexing under my touch. The heat of his body burning into mine, sunshine warming the ice in my heart he created when he left. And that's what scares me. Just this quickly, I'm consumed by him, the princess and the warrior, as he used to call us. My man. My hero. And those are dangerous things for me to feel, so very dangerous. Because they're not real. He showed me that they aren't real.

"This means nothing," I say, tearing my mouth from his, my hand planting on the hard wall of his chest. "This is sex. Just sex. This changes nothing."

"Baby, we were never just sex."

"We are not the us of the past," I say, grabbing his lapel. "I just need—you owe me this. You owe me a proper—"

"Everything," he says. "In ways you don't understand, but, baby, you will. I promise you, you will."

I don't try to understand that statement and I really don't get the chance. His mouth is back on my mouth.

The very idea of forever with this man is one part perfect, another part absolute pain. Because there is no forever with this man. But he doesn't give me time to object to a fantasy I'll never own, that I'm not sure I want to try and own again. I don't need forever. I need right now. I need him. I sink back into the kiss and he's ravenous. Claiming me. Taking me. Kissing the hell out of me and God, I love it. God, I need it. I need *him*.

FIND OUT MORE ABOUT THE SAVAGE SERIES HERE:

https://www.lisareneejones.com/savage-series.html

The Lilah Love Series

As an FBI profiler, it's Lilah Love's job to think like a killer. And she is very good at her job. When a series of murders surface—the victims all stripped naked and shot in the head—Lilah's instincts tell her it's the work of an assassin, not a serial killer. But when the case takes her back to her hometown in the Hamptons and a mysterious but unmistakable connection to her own life, all her assumptions are shaken to the core.

Thrust into a troubled past she's tried to shut the door on, Lilah's back in the town where her father is mayor, her brother is police chief, and she has an intimate history with the local crime lord's son, Kane Mendez. The two share a devastating secret, and only Kane understands Lilah's own darkest impulses. As more corpses surface, so does a series of anonymous notes to Lilah, threatening to expose her. Is the killer someone in her own circle? And is she the next target?

FIND OUT MORE ABOUT THE LILAH LOVE SERIES HERE:

https://www.lisareneejonesthrillers.com/the-lilah-love-series.html

Also by Lisa Renee Jones

THE INSIDE OUT SERIES

If I Were You
Being Me
Revealing Us
His Secrets*
Rebecca's Lost Journals
The Master Undone*
My Hunger*
No In Between
My Control*
I Belong to You
All of Me*

THE SECRET LIFE OF AMY BENSEN

Escaping Reality
Infinite Possibilities
Forsaken
Unbroken*

CARELESS WHISPERS

Denial
Demand
Surrender

WHITE LIES

Provocative
Shameless

TALL, DARK & DEADLY

Hot Secrets
Dangerous Secrets
Beneath the Secrets

WALKER SECURITY

Deep Under
Pulled Under
Falling Under

LILAH LOVE

Murder Notes
Murder Girl
Love Me Dead
Love Kills
Bloody Vows
Bloody Love (June 2021)

DIRTY RICH

Dirty Rich One Night Stand
Dirty Rich Cinderella Story
Dirty Rich Obsession
Dirty Rich Betrayal
Dirty Rich Cinderella Story: Ever After
Dirty Rich One Night Stand: Two Years Later
Dirty Rich Obsession: All Mine
Dirty Rich Secrets
Dirty Rich Betrayal: Love Me Forever

THE FILTHY TRILOGY

The Bastard
The Princess

The Empire

THE NAKED TRILOGY

One Man
One Woman
Two Together

THE SAVAGE SERIES

Savage Hunger
Savage Burn
Savage Love
Savage Ending

THE BRILLIANCE TRILOGY

A Reckless Note
A Wicked Song
A Sinful Encore

ADRIAN'S TRILOGY

When He's Dirty
When He's Bad
When He's Wild

*eBook only

About the Lisa Renee Jones

New York Times and USA Today bestselling author Lisa Renee Jones writes dark, edgy fiction to include the highly acclaimed INSIDE OUT series and the upcoming, crime thriller The Poet. Suzanne Todd (producer of Alice in Wonderland and Bad Mom's) on the INSIDE OUT series: Lisa has created a beautiful, complicated, and sensual world that is filled with intrigue and suspense.

Prior to publishing Lisa owned a multi-state staffing agency that was recognized many times by The Austin Business Journal and also praised by the Dallas Women's Magazine. In 1998 Lisa was listed as the #7 growing women owned business in Entrepreneur Magazine. She lives in Colorado with her husband, a cat that talks too much, and a Golden Retriever who is afraid of trash bags.

Lisa loves to hear from her readers. You can reach her at lisareneejones.com and she is active on Twitter and Facebook daily.